Previous novels by D. M. Samson

Silent Violence

In 1984 Dawn Marie travelled with her husband to Saudi Arabia. He had secured a job replacing the outgoing foreman of a secluded farm near Riyadh. Almost two years later she would return. Alone. Broken.

In *Silent Violence* she tells us of her journey: a long downward spiral. From the first inklings of things not being right, a pet killer in the expatriate compound, clandestine excursions by the farm crew, through to the rising hysteria within the expatriate community, then the killings at the farm, the ensuing imprisonment, moral deterioration, government procrastination and eventual deliverance.

Without question her story is harrowing. Yet it contains a great deal of humour too. For humour is the life jacket that keeps the displaced person buoyant in a strange culture.

After years of psychiatric treatment she was persuaded to write her story. The road to publication is a story in itself. Ultimately the book was suppressed in the interests of international relations.

Silent Violence should be a warning to prospective expatriates. Its portrayal of Arab mentality could help policy makers too.

Nails

There is little one can say about the plot. Succinctly put, it is the story of one day in the life of a car mechanic. Admittedly, not much in itself. But it's hard, raw, violent, sexy, sensitive, funny, poetic and philosophical to boot. It's a page-turner that grabs you by the short and curlies.

About the author

David M. Samson, born in Wallasey (near Liverpool) in 1957, lives with his wife and two daughters in Germany.

Bottle

Copyright © David M. Samson 2009

The right of David M. Samson to be identified as author of this work has been asserted in accordance with the Copyright, Designs and Patents Act 1988.

All rights reserved. No part of this work may be reproduced or stored in an information retrieval system (other than for purposes of review) without the express permission of the publisher in writing.

First published in 2009 by David M. Samson, 20 Arundel Road, Bath, Avon BA1 6EF.

Printed and bound by Lulu.com.
Lulu Enterprises Inc.
860 Aviation Parkway
Suite 300
Morrisville, NC 27560
United States of America

ISBN 978-0-9556796-2-9

British Library Cataloguing in Publication Data.
A catalogue record for this book is available from the British Library.

Cover design by David M. Samson.

www.davidmsamson.com

Life's but a walking shadow, a poor player,
That struts and frets his hour upon the stage,
And then he is heard no more; it is a tail
Told by an idiot, full of sound and fury,
Signifying nothing.
                    Macbeth, William Shakespeare

I write for the moment and prosperity.
Oops, sorry, of course I meant posterity.
                    Bottle, D.M. Samson

David M. Samson, January 2009

Many thanks to Bryan Johnson, without whose persistent badgering this book would never have been written.

Blame him.

The trill of the telephone wrenched him out of sleep. He was surprised to see that it was bright outside. A glance at the clock told him it was passed nine. He lay there for a moment wondering what had woken him.

He didn't have a hangover in a traditional sense. His head didn't ache, but he felt out of phase. And his stomach was a tumble-drier.

Then he heard the phone.

The phone hadn't awakened him in years now. Not since the break-in at Mick's.

"Kev. It's Martin."

"Yeah, what?" he had stammered. "It's dark. What time is it?"

"Three. Get over to Johnson's as soon as you can. The alarm's gone off at Mick's."

"Why are we meeting there?" Johnson's scrap yard was round the corner from the garage.

"Jeez Kev, think about it on the way. Bring something heavy." He had a crowbar under the front passenger car seat.

"What about the police?"

"They're on their way. Now fuck off and get going. Wait there for us. Mick and Kurt are on their way."

Yes, light-years ago.

He swung wearily out of bed. By the time he was standing the phone had jolted his nerves a third time. How long had it been ringing before rousing him? His answer-phone kicked in after twelve rings.

He pulled the bedroom door aside and strode across the lounge to the small table at his flat door.

"Yeah, yeah," he whispered under his breath as the phone rang for a fourth time.

He snatched up the hand-piece. "Yeah?"

"Hallo, Kevin."

"Hi Mum. What's up?"

"Kevin, I've got some bad news." She waited a moment before continuing. He was wide-awake. "I called last night, but you weren't in." The small red light was not blinking. She never left messages. He didn't understand it, but she didn't like the answer-phone. She said it put her in a tizz and she didn't know what to say.

"What is it Mum?"

"It's Sandra." His stomach clenched against the churning. "Kevin, she's been involved in an accident."

"Is she okay?"

"Oh Kevin." Was she crying? "No, she's not. She's been killed."

"Wha – You're – "

He was silent and she was too.

"How? What happened?"

"Her sister phoned me last night. You'd better phone her. As I understand it she got run over by a drunk driver. But I'm not sure I got it all. You'd better phone. Have you got her number?"

"Sandra," he had said, wanting her attention, "will you marry me?"

"Kevin?"

"Yes, Mum? Sorry I …"

He was naked and he suddenly felt cold. Very cold.

"Have you got her number?"

"Whose?"

"Sally's."

"Yes, I, er, think so. But you'd better give it to me just in case."

He scrawled the number on one of the scraps of paper beside the telephone. His hand was shaking and the paper slipped, so he wedged the telephone between his chin and shoulder and held the paper still.

"Are you going to be, okay?"

He held the phone again. "Yeah, yeah, fine Mum."

"Call a friend. You shouldn't be on your own." She knew he wouldn't travel across the country to her a day before work.

"Yes, Mum." Although, he couldn't think of anyone to call.

"You'd better phone Sally, then."

"Yes."

"Kevin, love you."

"Yeah, you too Mum." He hung up.

Although he felt cold, he didn't move. He stared at the phone. His Mum should have left a message. But what message could she have left? Phone me, at most. And would he have phoned her so late and in the state he had been in?

He looked at the dent in the door. His knuckles had taken the brunt, but it was the back of his hand that had ached for weeks afterwards. The punch was to vent his anger after an argument early in his relationship with Sandra. Kevin looked back into the lounge and then at the number he had scrawled.

"It's Sandra. Kevin, she's been involved in an accident."

He made an effort to see her and was aghast that he could only partially visualise her and then only fleetingly.

Why hadn't his Mum just come out with it? Why the solemn introduction? Of course he knew the answer. It was her way. The only way she knew. She hadn't wanted to be dramatic. Yes, and she had wanted him to brace himself. But some part of her didn't want to come out with it. She couldn't accept it. Just as some part of her recoiled from using the answer-phone.

He was being stupid, of course. How would he have come out with it?

Shit. She was dead. Sandra was dead. He'd never see her again. Never hear her laughter. Her voice. Feel her skin. See the freckles on her arm. The mole in the small of her back.

And more than two years ago they had been naked in the bedroom. The room was charged with emotion. He was very upset.

She said: "If this is love, then I'm very disappointed."

He cried silently and she did the same. Crying they had

tenderly made love on the bed.

Kevin grew angry at the memory. He didn't want it. He wanted to remember her well. He wanted the good times.

He took a deep breath and his side flared. "You and whose fuckin' army?"

"Fuck off," he hissed into the empty flat.

He strode across the lounge, seeing his scratchings on the writing pad on the dining table. He'd title it "What the fuck!" This was his attempt at making sense of nonsense.

"Shit," he said as he went to the chest of drawers in the bedroom. He pulled out a pair of boxer shorts and climbed into them. Then he went over and tore back the curtains. The light flooded the room but didn't dispel the emptiness, the huge silence.

"Oh Kevin. No, she's not. She's been killed."

"Wha – You're – " And he'd almost said in reflex: "you're joking." Luckily it hadn't come out.

He went to the toilet, lifted the seat and stood for a moment. Then he changed his mind and sat. He watched a silverfish run the rim of the bath at the tiles, before disappearing down an ancient crack. There was a time when most of the edge of the bath, no, the entire bathroom, was chocker with cosmetic bottles and tubes of all shapes and sizes. It had smelt like Boots the chemist. He had worried that the perfume would stick and the boys at work would think he was a poof. He'd joked in front of Sandra that he had trouble finding his toothbrush. Once, when she was out he'd accidentally knocked a bottle over whilst drying himself and it had been like those standing dominoes, one knocking the next. And when he came to right them, he was too clumsy or his hands were too big and one was forever toppling the other, frustration eventually stealing his smile.

Kevin wiped his bum, pulled up his underwear, covered and flushed the toilet, washed his hands with soap and dried them on a towel.

Then he was standing over the phone again. This time he was in striped boxer shorts. The bruise at his side was still purple, but it was no longer so intense. Brawling over a woman in the pub. Clever, real clever. The silence made him uncomfortable, but then he didn't want to be comfortable.

Kevin saw the depression in the floorboard near the door. To see herself in the full-length mirror whilst on the telephone, Sandra had stretched the cord across width of the flat door and the phone crash down. Since then something rattled in the phone, but it worked perfectly.

He picked up the hand-piece and dialled the number.

The last time he'd seen Sally was when she had stayed with Sandra. He remembered the three of them in his Triumph Spitfire. It was about eleven at night. Sandra was beside him; Sally crammed in the back. A car was tailing them through empty suburbia. He'd speeded up, took extra turns and he'd tapped the break pedal. Still the car stuck to him. His mind raced. Sally couldn't see out of the oval back window. Only by chance on a turn was the distance enough for him to see in his wing mirror the coloured glass adorning the top of the car. "Shit. It's the police," he said quietly and pulled over.

The phone was picked up in the middle of the second ring, almost as if the person had been waiting for the call.

"Hallo?"

"Sally. It's Kevin."

"Kevin." He could hear the gurgling of a baby. "Just a minute." Then, presumably to her husband. "Take him." He could hear her breathing. "Kevin?"

"Yes."

"You know?"

"Yes, my Mum told me. Just now. But –"

"What?" She was again speaking off-phone. "No, look, mummy's on the phone. Ask daddy. Tim, please."

Kevin knew she had a young child; the baby was a new addition.

"Sorry, Kevin." She paused to gather herself. "I couldn't find your number, but I found your Mum's. I hope –"

"It was okay."

"I thought you'd want to come to the funeral. It's, er, on Wednesday."

"Yes, of course."

"I'll give you the address. Have you got a pen and paper?"

"Yes." He wrote down the details of where and when.

"Sally, er, my Mum was a bit vague about what happened. Can you tell me?"

She was silent. Was she shocked?

"Yes." But the word was very small, almost a whisper. And Kevin suddenly realised her hurt.

"If you can't it's okay. I –"

"No, Kevin. You should know." But her words were measured. "Do you mind if Tim tells you?"

"Of course not. I –"

"I'll give you him now." And she was talking off-phone again, her hand over the mouthpiece, muffling the instructions to her husband.

"Hi Kevin," said Tim as if they were best buddies. But Kevin had only met him once and they'd exchanged a mere handful of words. Tim had been the newcomer sitting behind Sally, who was herself on the edge of an established group.

"Hi, Tim."

"How are you?"

"Fine. Just tell me how it happened."

"It was all a dumb accident," he began. "Wednesday. Brian said they came out of the disco and were going for the bus at the high street. Where you ever here?"

"Yes."

"You know at the lights by HMV?"

"Yeah, I know where you mean." Who was Brian?

"He said they were red, but later he said they were about to change. Definitely amber. It doesn't matter, I suppose. He got across okay, but she was following. And this drunken idiot didn't see her and thought he could get across the lights." Tim fell silent. "Kevin?"

"I'm here," he said quietly. But Tim was silent. "They get the driver?"

"Yeah, after hitting her he went straight into the lights opposite. Cracked his head on his steering wheel. Brian said he wanted to pull him out and give him a pasting. But there was blood all over his face and the people from the bus stop had come over. I think the bus driver called for help." He paused. "She didn't suffer. It was instant."

Kevin tried to visualise the accident. He tried to see her hurt and broken, lying on the hard road, her face cover in blood. He tried to feel her hurt. He didn't want it. He didn't want any of it. "He got across okay, but she was following." Why wasn't he with her? Why wasn't it him? Wanker.

"Kevin?"

"Yeah, Tim, sorry. It's a little hard to take."

"Yeah," he said, beginning to talk like Kevin. "I'm sorry, mate."

"Yeah." It sounded as though Tim had placed his hand over the mouthpiece. He couldn't hear the children in the background. Then he could hear them and Tim said: "Kevin, I'm sorry, I've got to go. You're coming on Wednesday?"

"Yes."

"We'll see you then."

"Yeah."

"Bye."

"Bye."

After replacing the receiver the silence was overwhelming.

Again he stood looking at nothing in particular. He looked into the lounge. On the table was his letter to his aunt abandoned to the scrawlings of a slobbering drunkard.

"Wednesday," Tim had said. What had he been doing on Wednesday? He couldn't remember. Why had he only just heard? He should have heard earlier. He would have liked to have heard earlier. But they'd been apart for more than two years now. He had a letter somewhere. From about nine months ago. Why the fuck hadn't he replied? There exchange of Christmas cards with promises of newsy letters to follow had been merely a ritual. Shit. It was all shit.

What had he been doing on Wednesday? He'd certainly been asleep when she was killed. The next day he'd gone to work as usual. And the day had been like any other.

He knew the high street and the lights at HMV. He could see it in his mind's eye. And he tried to imagine what happened. He found himself again trying to visualise Sandra, bloodied and broken on the road. But the idea was horrible and, thankfully, the image wouldn't come. At best he saw her asleep.

"It's Matthew, isn't it?" he ventured.

Sandra said nothing.

"Isn't it?"

"Nothing's happened."

"You want something to happen?"

Again she said nothing.

"Well?"

"I don't know."

"Yes, you do."

"Kevin, don't."

"Don't what?"

"Just don't."

Pause.

"You do want something to happen."

"Okay, yes. Is that what you want to hear?"

"Fine. Bloody fine." He was tumbling. "Well go ahead. Take it. Do what the fuck you want!"

"But I don't know. Don't you see?"

"All I see is that you don't want me."

"Kevin," she pleaded. "I don't know what I want."

"Fine. Well, I'm making the decision for you."

She was silent, her eyes cast downwards.

"Okay?"

Then she nodded.

The questions started slowly, but gathered momentum the more he thought about the accident. Had the lights really been green? Who was Brian? And why hadn't he waited for Sandra? Bastard. Why hadn't it been him? Was it the driver who had been drunk or had it been them? Had she suffered? Instant, he said. Instant. Like switching off a light.

And he thought of making himself a coffee: his kick-start to the morning. That was instant too. Instant. Instant. The word repeated itself in his head until it became meaningless.

Sandra stepped away from the counter with him. She was a little wobbly after the pub. He'd stepped down to the tables and eating area. But she'd been too engrossed in selecting a chip and missed the step. She yelped and her chips leapt from the newspaper straight up into the air. They landed all about her and she stood holding the newspaper and greased bag with a few sorry survivors. She roared with laughter. Kevin did too.

He became aware of his churning stomach. Hopefully it wasn't going to advance into spin.

Could he phone Sally again? He wanted answers. He could ask to talk to Tim. No. He couldn't phone again. It'd have to keep until Wednesday.

"It's Matthew, isn't it?" he ventured.

He would probably be at the funeral. Or maybe not. Matt the prat he'd called him. He hadn't lasted long. But Sandra had not come back. That annoyed him. He'd made no effort to get her back. Maybe he should have. And so she ended up with some guy called Brian crossing the high street just as the lights were about to change and a drunk thought he could jump them.

What had been doing last Wednesday? He'd stayed in. Yes, he'd come straight home. That was day he'd spent all afternoon replacing a pair of front suspension lever dampers. And he'd been fit for nothing other than flopping in front of the television. He remembered watching the *Benny Hill Show*. He was in bed by eleven. So, he'd been asleep when she died.

If they'd stayed together and had the kid, would they, after a few years, have been at each other's throats? And would she have been taken from him last Wednesday, because her number was up? It was all madness.

The silence in the flat was so complete he could hear its movement, as if the flat were alive: a tick, sometimes a crack, all swallowed by the emptiness. Outside the birds were whistling. Someone far off was mowing a lawn too. Things were continuing in their mundane way. Whereas his flat was a mausoleum. Time stood still.

He needed noise too. He needed music to fill the air. But he made no attempt to go to his stereo. Instead he went into the kitchen. He checked the kettle for enough water and switched it on. He then spooned two heaped teaspoons of Nescafé into a mug.

The plastic bowl in the sink was full of dirty dishes. He sighed. Then, holding the crockery with spread fingers he tipped the bowl to get rid of the dirty water. Cutlery slipped through and clanged into the stainless steel sink. The grey water washed over them and the crockery shifted dangerously over his hand. Satisfied that he'd drained away most of the water he put the bowl down on the draining board and returned the cutlery to it. The whole affair was placed into the sink; a mug within was given two squirts of washing up liquid, before the hot tap was blasted onto it.

A poem from the book Helen had lent him sprung to mind.

The scar

The scar is
old skin

Old skin is
dead skin

Dead skin is
dust

Dust to be blown

When he read it, he wanted to kid himself into believing this was how he felt about Sandra.

He thought he'd got over Sandra leaving, but now he had to get over her leaving all over again.

An ant on the windowsill caught his attention. It was investigating the one he'd crushed the previous day to Echo and the Bunnymen's *The Cutter*. The insect left and returned, fussed about the dead one. It seemed frantic, checking the area like a bloodhound. Kevin watched it until the bowl was full. Then when it was far enough away he used the damp sponge to wipe the dead one into the gap between the bowl and the sink.

The water under the bubbles was too hot and the kettle hadn't boiled. He noticed a sparrow perched on the branch of the neighbour's tree.

Kevin was at the curtains looking out at nothing. His mother and his youngest sister, Rosie, were sobbing behind him. His other sister and two brothers hadn't arrived. He wasn't crying. He was stone. Stone cold. But not dead. Not like his father behind him. He'd seen a sparrow then. It had landed on the window ledge, unaware of his presence, on the other side of the glass. For a while, as it jerked its head sideways this way and that, he watched it for a sign. He wanted it to be his Dad with a message that everything was all right. And he remembered one of the two stupid things his Dad had said. This one was: "when your number's up, it's up." And echoes of boating as a boy with his father were inextricably linked to this sentence. Like the man with the hand-held loudhailer: "Come in number sixteen. Your time is up." All so routine and mundane. So depressingly little for the end of a life. Of course, in the last weeks his father had said nothing. With his wasting body communication had deteriorated to the squeeze of a hand, the movement of a finger.

The kettle rocked and bumped and snapped off. He waited until the noise was a memory before pouring the water into the mug.

He opened the wall unit and fetched the box of Weetabix. He took down a bowl and then picked a spoon from the drawer. Even though he only placed one brick in the bowl - normally he ate two or three - he wondered whether he could finish it. He opened the bag of sugar and sprinkled some on top. This was the only time he used sugar. Normally it was in the flat for guests.

The shame of his father's death was that a part of him had wanted him to die. His deterioration was torture to watch. Especially for his Mum. She aged visibly. An instant death meant no goodbyes, but a drawn out one was no better. The sickness reduced his father to a cornered animal, the skin of his face clawed back to all teeth and eyes. Of course Kevin hadn't wished for him to die. But as the weeks went on he wanted an end to it. An end for everybody's sake.

He felt guilty that he'd not thought of his father for some time. "Don't mourn for me for too long. Get on with your life. Enjoy your life. Be happy."

"Kevin," his Mum began, "now I know what your Dad said about taking care of me. Well, I'll be fine. I'll be happier when I know you've found somebody. I though it was that girl -"

"Mum."

"All right. But I want you to get on with your life, just as your Dad said. Don't worry about me."

His Mum lived alone. He had the impression she was continually trying to fill her empty world. A world as empty as his was now. And even if her world wasn't empty, then it was quiet.

Once her world had been loud and full. Over full. A family of seven living on top of each other in the three-bedroom terraced house: Dad, Mum, Gary, Ian, Kevin, Maggie and Rosie. Physically it was a squeeze. His parents slept in the back bedroom, the three boys in the front. The two girls were crammed in the box bedroom with a bunk bed and a large wardrobe.

Living so close the children had learnt sharing. And they learnt much more than this.

With only one television they had learnt democracy and

bowel-control. The democracy came through deciding what was to be watched. A vote was taken. And there being five of them meant that a decision was always reached. Naturally it wasn't as straight forward as that. Sometimes there was an "I don't mind" that caused a deadlock. Other times there was bickering, with accusations of votes being bought through promises of play.

The bowel-control came through sitting through the television programmes without leaving a prized seat. Certain viewing positions were coveted and if left would immediately be taken.

Now he felt guilty because he was not thinking about Sandra. Or was he feeling guilty because he was living and she was not? Thinking about her would not bring her back.

"You've done well there," said Mick. They'd had the slap-up meal and now they were in some club. His boss was rolling drunk. They were all drunk. It was the Christmas bash.

"Well, you can't have a piece," he said. And Mick roared.

After sniffing the carton Kevin poured the milk on his cereal and took it to the dining table in the lounge. His writing paper and pen were unceremoniously shoved aside. He sat and spooned a mouthful into his mouth and began chewing. He didn't really need to chew, but he did and he did it without relish, chewing longer than usual, as if swallowing would be painful.

He saw the tail end of his ranting on the paper.

You want meaninglessness? I say, what the fuck. Because great if you've got meaning, tough if you haven't, but in the end you sit back and it all ends with a smile: What the fuck.

You fucking idiot, he thought. And he picked the pad up and turned it over.

"Call a friend. You shouldn't be on your own."

Ah, but Kevin would be on his own. Yes, he longed to tell someone. The only people who sprung to mind were John and Lyn. They'd been around during his time with Sandra. On occasion they'd been a foursome. But he'd all but lost contact with them when they moved up North. Then there were Tony and Brenda. They'd made up a foursome too. But they'd broken up. And Tony remained an uneasy acquaintance, more Chris's friend. It was the girls who had bonded. And Brenda had upped and left to God knows where.

Kevin wasn't sure whether he wanted to tell people who vaguely knew Sandra because he wanted them to suffer. Maybe he wanted sympathy. He wasn't sure.

"You look really handsome," she smiled.

He was in his best togs. She in hers.

Kevin laughed. "Sandra, it's almost pitch black in here." But he was pleased.

It was her birthday and they were sitting in a posh restaurant. The tables were candlelit. The diners talked quietly and the waiters moved about on their toes.

He'd decided against beer with the courses they had chosen. Beer bloated. But when the food came, the portions were disappointingly small for the money. There were gaps on the plate. They drunk wine. But he didn't know wine and he drank it like water and he'd ordered a second carafe. They'd spent the entire evening there. And by the time they were finished he felt painfully full. The food had been heavy like the napkins. He'd been groggy when she slid the card across the linen as they waited for the bill. It was from the restaurant. He turned it over to see what she'd written. Three words in her bubbly handwriting. There was a small x at the end like a full stop. "I love you too," he said and they held hands across the table until the waiter arrived.

He took another mouthful of cereal. She'd never eat again. His stomach flipped, but he controlled it.

Was Brian a friend or boyfriend? Wednesday was a funny day to go to a disco.

The sound of metal upon crockery jarred and he put the spoon down. He'd not eaten very much. Less than half. He looked at it. It looked like soggy cardboard. He was repulsed. The thought of eating repulsed him. Like when they were leaving that posh restaurant and people were receiving their meals.

He sat there for a while. He had planned to go to the gym. But now he couldn't. In fact he didn't know what to do. So he just sat there.

He imagined being at the funeral, which made him think of his Dad's funeral. He'd been the rear left pall bearer. Lots of old people had been there. Aunts and uncles he barely recognised from his youth. There were work colleagues too. And Kevin realised that he had not really known his father. Not really known him as a person. He'd known him only as a father. Showing his fatherly face like a politician shows a political face. By the time he reached a discerning age and could get to know his father he was wrapped up in his own world and he'd left home.

The clock showed that it was after ten. He saw his abandoned cereal. It had soaked up all the milk and looked like a lump of cardboard papier-mâché. No doubt it tasted like it too.

Then he remembered the dishes. He got up and took the bowl to the kitchen. There he scraped the sludge into the flip-top bin. He slipped the bowl and spoon in the dishwater. It was still warm.

But now he didn't want the silence. He considered the radio. No. Too dangerous. Who knows what might come up?

He went back into the lounge and crouched at his records. He hadn't changed over to CDs yet. He knew he eventually would. Vinyl was on its way out. But some of his collection simply wasn't available on CD. And probably never would be.

There was no way Leonard Cohen's *No way to say goodbye* was going on the turntable. She'd introduced him to the singer-songwriter. No way. So it was goodbye to Leonard Cohen for a while.

As he looked through his collection he was surprised by the number of records he couldn't play. There were her records, his records and their records. Hers were Blondie and Roxy Music. Theirs were Cohen, Bowie, Bob Marley and the Rolling Stones. His were Joy Division, The Waterboys, Pink Floyd, The Clash, The Stranglers, The Jam and The Boomtown Rats. She had given him the latter as a birthday present.

He decided upon *Snap!* The Jam.

He slipped the first record from its sleeve, placed it on the turntable, switched the player on and lowered the stylus.

The music smashed into the air and it took a moment for Kevin to suppress the urge to return to silence.

Normally Paul Weller's voice and the urgency of the music mobilised him. *In the City* had him jumping about, punching the air. If not physically, then at least mentally. But the music didn't reach him. It was flat, meaningless background noise as inspiring as his wallpaper.

He went back into the kitchen and mechanically began to wash the dishes. Try as he might he couldn't get into the music. It kept slipping into background noise.

"Kevin," his father shouted. "Turn that bloody racket down. You'll go deaf."

"What?"

"I said –" And Kevin laughed. And his father had too.

"Keep it down, son."

The second stupid thing his Dad had said was after he'd been diagnosed as having stomach cancer. "It's just one of those things, son." One of what things? What a bland and meaningless thing to say.

Three words in her bubbly handwriting with a small x at the end like a full stop. And at the time she had loved him. At the time. Did anyone love consistently? His Mum and Dad had argued and made-up, argued and made-up. Maybe love came and went like energy or enthusiasm.

The Jam were thrashing away at the *Modern World*.

His hand swept the bottom of the bowl searching for that last teaspoon. They had a knack of hiding themselves, slipping out like a canoe in a waterfall when he tipped the water out of the bowl into the sink. There he had it.

The tear on Sandra's face was a shock. He'd been grave before the operation, but she'd been practical and almost light-hearted. Breezy, he'd say. After the operation he'd noticed moments like this. Of course he couldn't miss the tear. The previous hints as to how it had affected her had been slight disputable things. This was indisputable. But he couldn't question her, because he was on top of her. She asked him to come and he balanced a tightrope between obeying and rolling off her. Before the operation they'd done it everywhere. They couldn't keep their hands off each other. Outside a pub, in the car, beyond a lay-by after stopping to remove a stone from a tyre, slow and quiet with Sally in the next room, on a train. That same lust that had driven them then was at play here. And yet, something had changed. He always wondered whether this was the turning point. Whether this big silent tear edging down her face was the moment at which her love for him began to diminish.

This was his worst image of Sandra.

He stopped and looked out of the window. There was no bird on the tree.

"There's nothing mysterious about seeing dead people," he had said to Sally. She had been talking about a reading of the Tarot.

Sandra looked at him questioningly too.

"I see them all the time."

They were hooked. He took a sup of his beer, savouring it and the moment.

"You do too."

"How's that then?" asked Sandra like a challenge.

He smiled.

"Film."

The girls groaned. And he chuckled at their disappointment.

It all seemed stupid now. But he wasn't interested in the occult. He was sceptical of talk of anything supernatural. That star sign poppycock was the worst. At work, for a laugh, they took turns in reading out their horoscopes. Some daily rags were better than others. But nearly all carried better horoscopes than jokes.

Kevin was uneasy with borderline phenomenon. Inexplicable things that defied his reason had to be ignored.

Death was in this category. And he couldn't ignore it. It was in his face.

Certain that the bowl was empty he tipped the water out. It gushed dangerously high, threatening to swamp the dishes arranged on the draining board. No teaspoon this time. He put the bowl upon the draining water and for a moment it rocked like a dingy.

He remembered Helen. He could phone her. But what could he say? He'd seen her only yesterday. Somehow he knew she wouldn't be keen to see him. Even under these circumstances. And who knows what he might say or do? With her he had to have his wits about him. At the moment he was barely holding himself together.

He dried the dishes with a teacloth and put them away until the end of the record interrupted him. At the stereo he turned the record over, realising that he hadn't listened to any of it. Oh, the music had been there, but he had not heard it.

The second side was as disruptive as the first, but he didn't want silence.

He went back to drying the remaining dishes and wondered what he should do next. A glance at the kitchen clock told him it was 10:22. The whole day lay before him.

Should he call Helen?

"It's funny, but no one knows what to say when you mention death." Kevin allowed himself to take Helen into his confidence. For a few moments the easy, witty Kevin disappeared. "When an ex-girlfriend of mine was killed in a car crash, no one knew what to say." He was speaking of a girl he had met after his relationship with Sandra, in the wake of which he had not taken seriously. Only after she had left him did he realise what he had thrown away. She had earned his respect and he'd just begun to show an interest in her when she was killed. "It certainly hammered home the frailty of life..."

Andrea had been her name. He regretted not naming her. But naming other women, no matter if they were dead, was a mechanism he'd curbed with Helen. She was his project. He didn't want to risk alienating her with talk of past conquests.

Conquest? Hardly. He'd bedded Andrea only once. And he'd been rubbish. What had she said when he later began to show interest? "You made me feel cheap." Yes, he had. His only excuse was that he was on the rebound after Sandra.

Like his father Andrea too had left words that had lodged in his mind; splinters under his skin. That morning as they lay in bed together he had moaned about his routine. He knew he had overdone it, probably presenting it as a rut, because she said: "If you don't like something, change it." Yeah, he had thought, easier said than done.

She'd turned his bedside clock around. She wouldn't be dictated by time, she said. And that too fitted with her hedonistic nature.

He opened the utensil drawer, a knife and the tea towel in his hand. He saw the corkscrew immediately. How often had he opened the drawer and not noticed it? The number of times it had been used could be counted on the fingers of one hand. Wine wasn't his thing. The corkscrew was an iron figure of the devil or a demon with short horns. It was dark, almost black, contrasting the shiny-chromed look of the rest of the contents of the drawer. Its penis was the corkscrew. Vicious. In a fist it was a hell of a dangerous weapon. Serious damage stuff.

"The alarm's gone off at Mick's... Bring something heavy."

"What about the police?"

"They're on their way. Now fuck off and get going. Wait there for us. Mick and Kurt are on their way."

Mick and Kurt were already at Johnson's yard when he arrived. Martin arrived moments later. There was nobody about.

"Okay," said Mick. "I don't want heroics. Let's go in quietly. There may be more of them than us."

"Shouldn't we wait for the police?" Kurt asked.

Mick couldn't hide his exasperation. "We could wait until I'm cleaned out and there's no garage to go to on Monday. I won't be the first to be laid off."

"Let's get going," said Martin.

"If the police are there, don't let them see what you're carrying." Mick held up his King Dick 7/8" Whitworth brute of a fourteen-inch spanner. No messing.

The corkscrew was a memento from their holiday in Greece. Sandra and he had spent two weeks together on a Corfu beach. It really had been a beach holiday. Like the cocktails they drank their relationship was on the rocks. During the day they were separate people, hiding behind hangovers, lolling about in the sun, sleeping, reading. For they only came together and had sex when they were blotto. They didn't make love. They had sex. And the number of times could be counted on one hand with fingers to spare. It was a terrible holiday. But it had been booked and they'd both put money into it when their relationship was good. To cancel would mean the loss of their hefty deposit. They chose to pay the full whack and have a painful holiday.

The last teaspoon was dried and put away.

He flicked the kettle on for another coffee. Opening the drawer he probably picked out the teaspoon he'd just dried. So what? He heaped coffee into a mug. And stood waiting for the kettle to boil.

He could do some ironing. And later he could get a video to fill the evening. There was nothing on the box.

First he'd have a shower and get dressed.

The kettle boiled and he waited a tick before pouring water into his mug. He left it and went to the bedroom. He had an urge to get out the shoebox of photos and look through them. There were some from that holiday. Most were either of him or her alone. But there was one some tourist had taken for them. They had their arms around each other and were smiling like a couple. It was a good photograph, even if it was a lie.

He opened the chest of drawers for some socks. Picked his jeans off the floor and found a T-shirt that didn't whiff draped over the end of the bed. As he carried it all to the bathroom the buckle jingled. His thick leather belt with the etchings of warriors, with shields and swords, was also from their Greek holiday.

So many things tied her to him.

He checked the progress of the record before closing the bathroom door.

After heaping his clothes on the lid of the wash-basket and stepping out of his boxer shorts, he climbed into the bath, pulled the shower curtain across, hiding the sight of his anguished face in the mirror of the medicine cabinet above the sink. He had decided to forego shaving. He was shampooing his hair when he heard the ringing. He froze with his fingers buried in his soapy hair. Yes, it was the phone. He rinsed his hair as fast as he could, switched off the shower, pulled back the curtain, grabbed a towel and rubbing himself as he opened the door, cursed at the water he was dripping everywhere, turned down the stereo and dived for the phone.

In the second before snatching it up he thought of who it could be. His Mum? Tim? Sally?

As soon as he saw that he was being tailed by the police he pulled over. He could understand that it was too late for them to use their siren. But why hadn't they put on their emergency lights? Or simply flashed him?

He got out, hoping in vain that the officer wouldn't look in the car and see that his two-seater carried three.

"What's up?" he asked casually.

He thought of explaining that he would have stopped earlier if they hadn't stuck so close. But his explanation could be taken the wrong way.

"Can I see your license, sir?"

"Sure," he said tugging his wallet out of his back pocket.

The officer moved passed him to look into the car. A second officer got out of the car, but didn't come over.

"Evening ladies."

"Evening officer," they chorused.

Kevin held out his driving license. The officer looked at it under torchlight.

After a moment he handed it back.

"Your rear lights aren't working. That's why we stuck close to you."

"It's probably a blown fuse," said Kevin.

"Have you a spare?"

"No. But we're almost home."

The officer asked him where he lived and said that they'd follow him most of the way. He made Kevin promise to get the light fixed. Without commenting on the extra passenger he returned to the police car.

"Yeah?" he said into the mouthpiece.

"Hi, Kevin, it's Kurt."

"Who – Wha- Kurt?"

"Yes, have you forgotten me? Pig-dog." Pig-dog was Kevin's joke: his literal translation of *Schweinehund*.

"Kurt, you old bugger. What's happening?" He wedged the telephone between his neck and shoulder and tried to adjust the towel about him. He was dripping water onto the notepaper.

"I've been over for the weekend. I was visiting my Mum. I'm flying back this evening. I thought I might pop by."

"Yeah? Great."

"That didn't sound convincing."

"No. I'm, er, freezing my pecker off here. You caught me under the shower."

There was a silence.

"Kevin, it is okay if something is happening. If you are busy I –"

"Leave it out, you old git. When can you be here?"

"That's better." He sounded relieved. "It'll be easier to meet at the usual. Say midday? Can you phone the others?"

"Yeah, sure." But he was not sure.

"Be there or be square. Hey, Kevin." He laughed and Kevin smiled. Nobody said that. Only a foreigner like Karl would come out with it. Burk. "See you."

"Yeah, see ya, Kurt."

He raced back to the shower. Only when he was again shampooing his hair did he remember the stereo. He cursed. He wasn't really cursing about the record playing mutely on. He cursed about having to play the bush drums. Phoning around wouldn't be as bad as going to the pub, though. They only had his voice and he could be brusque. But at the pub there was no hiding. No hiding the anguish in his face.

Who would he call? Mick? Yes. Steve? Yes. Chris? Yes. Tony? No. Al? Maybe. Ian? No. All the others had moved on. Martin, Greasy.

He should have told Kurt the truth. He could then have come to the flat. They could have talked. That would have been easier than exposure. Of course he could choose to forget phoning around. He could meet Kurt alone. They could have one drink and come back to the flat. But no. He couldn't let Kurt down. Call the others and let them meet Kurt? He could tell Chris or Steve – whoever was going – that something had come up. Again no. He couldn't let Kurt down. They hadn't seen him in years. Kevin had seen him more recently and that was over two years ago, after Sandra.

Kurt had never known Sandra. He'd left for Germany before they met. But he knew of Sandra. After the split Kevin had visited him in Hamburg. There in some seedy back street *Kneipe*, the tail end of a beer-swilling, cigar-smoking evening, taking in a sex-show on the *Reeperbahn*, Kevin had poured out his soul. He hadn't intended to speak about Sandra it simply came out. And once the floodgates were open it all came out. With anyone else Kevin would have subsequently been embarrassed. But Kurt and he went back a long way.

"We're with the convention," the eighteen-year-old Kevin said.

"What convention's that, then?" said the landlord, turning the check-in book round for them to sign-in. "The Bible society?" he scoffed. "I'll take the money up front."

Kurt and Kevin opened their wallets and handed him the cash for one night.

The old man perked up. "I've had some stay and scarper without paying."

He turned and took a set of keys from a hook on the wall behind him. The guesthouse didn't seem large enough to warrant so many room keys. Perhaps there was an extension at the back. Then he eyed them. "No strangers after ten. Okay?"

"Yes," said Kevin, before Kurt could say anything.

"Check out Sunday by eleven."

"Okay," said Kevin taking the keys.

"The door facing you at the end of the corridor."

They picked up their holdalls and went to the room. Two single beds lined the walls. A single chest of drawers separated the headboards and acted as a bedside table. Although, there was only one lamp with a worn flowery shade with gold coloured tassels. The room looked tired and shabby. Pulling back the curtains on the sash window they were confronted by a brick wall.

"No sea view, then," said Kevin. And they roared with laughter. More at the sordidness than the remark.

When they'd calmed Kurt said: "We can't bring women back here."

"You worried about that ten o'clock stuff?"

"No. I mean it is not nice here."

"Not nice," Kevin laughed. "You see any rats here?"

Kurt swept the room with his eyes. "No."

"Exactly. This place is below them."

They chuckled.

"I wouldn't worry about it. Let's get our stuff unpacked and get out of here. I'm hungry and we have to choose the best place." Then Kevin added with a sly smile: "Anyway, it'll be dark when we bring them back and they'll have other things on their mind."

He switched off the shower and climbed out of the bath. Snatching the bath towel he rubbed himself furiously. Then he dressed. Back in the lounge he checked the size of the small puddles as he walked over to the stereo. The record had finished.

He returned the stylus arm to its cradle and switched it off. He then plugged in the hairdryer at the socket near the flat door and full-length mirror.

Kevin managed to dry his hair without really seeing himself. Oh, he caught glimpses, but his hand and tufts of hair obstructed a head on collision.

When he switched off the hairdryer the flat plunged into silence.

He wasn't sure about putting on a record. After all, he had phone calls to make.

In the kitchen he sipped his coffee and thought about what he would say. On the pretext of calling others he could keep all the conversations short.

He looked at the clock 10:58. Thirty-six minutes on from when he last looked. More importantly he had about forty minutes before he'd have to leave for the pub. And he had to give the others some warning.

He took his coffee to the telephone. Then he fetched a dining chair. He had to look up Mick's phone number. Although Mick was his boss he was a lad. He ran the garage from his small office, but he mucked in and got his hands dirty when necessary. And then he advised, but didn't dictate. He let them get on with it. And he made sure the atmosphere was good without being intrusive. Sometimes he'd have a puzzle for them.

"What's the difference between illegal and breaking the law?"

And they'd be guessing for the best part of the morning. The serious answers giving way to the more bizarre or downright comical as time went on.

Eventually they'd given up and in the lunch break Mick had put them out of their misery.

"Breaking the law," he began learnedly, "is when you do something against the law." He paused, enjoying their attentiveness. "Whereas ill eagle is a sick bird."

This was met with groans and laughter.

"I've got a good mind to quit," said Kevin.

Yes, Mick was one of them at work. But outside work was another matter. Apart from being older than his workers, he was married with two small kids. His social circles, whatever they were, did not overlap with theirs. When he left work on a Friday they wouldn't see him again until Monday morning. Unless there was a big job that meant weekend overtime. Of course there was at least one exception that sprang to mind.

When the four of them arrived at the garage there was no one about and all looked in order. Then they saw that the lock of the yard gate had been smashed off. And the alarm box high on the garage wall was missing.

Kevin gave his crowbar a reassuring squeeze.

Mick pushed the gate quietly aside and led the way into the yard. The cars looked untouched and none appeared to be missing.

The alarm lay at the foot of the building covered in quick-setting foam. Evidently the foam hadn't been enough to still it and the burglars had torn it from the wall. They didn't know that it was linked to the police station.

Kevin saw movement behind a car. He signalled Martin who touched Mick. Kevin gestured and Mick pointed out a route for each of them.

Weapons at the ready they made their way between the cars.

Kevin let the phone ring ten times. It was a limit he had set. No answer-phone swung into action and he hung up.

He was relieved. Mick fleetingly knew Sandra.

"You've done well there," said Mick.

"Well, you can't have a piece." And Mick roared.

And Kevin had looked over and assessed Sandra from afar. She looked gorgeous. And she glanced over and saw him watching her. Her smile was full and beautiful. It filled him up and he swelled with joy and couldn't help beaming back.

Sadness engulfed him and he looked into his coffee. Would he cry? He wanted to, but he felt angry instead.

He got up. Then he went to the kitchen and stood at the window. The clouds drifted across the sky. They were beautiful against the blue. An airliner was leaving a vapour trail as it moved silent as a snail. A memory of the flight to Greece tried to surface and he pushed it down.

He quickly returned to the phone. Steve picked up on the fourth ring.

"Hallo?"

"Hi Steve."

"Oh, hi Kev."

"Listen. Kurt's here. Do you fancy meeting up?"

"Where?"

"Where do you think?"

"That'll be three days in a row."

"Who's counting?"

"Maybe we should buy ourselves a partnership with Terry. The -"

"Sorry Steve, I haven't got time I -"

"Are you all right, Kev? You sound -"

"Yep. Be there for twelve. I've got others to phone."

"Okay. But I -"

"I'm phoning Chris now. Okay?"

"I'll be there."

"Good."

He hung up.

That didn't go well. He had thought he could get away with it on the phone. Wrong.

Kevin picked up his coffee and sat there listening to the silence. The lawnmower had stopped. He could hear kids somewhere. The birds were making a racket.

He was going to phone Chris next, but decided to call Al instead. He knew Al wouldn't come. Oh, he'd like to see Kurt after all this time, but he would not feel comfortable in the pub. It wasn't a white pub and Terry wouldn't tolerate racism. But the pub attracted a certain clientele and because of this outsiders, especially blacks, didn't feel at home.

"Hey, Kev, what's happening?"

"Kurt's in town."

"Kermit? Well, fuck me - "

"Not while -"

"There're dogs on the street. Get yourself some new knee-jerk phrases, man."

"Yeah, yeah. I've got to phone Chris. We're meeting at the usual. You want to come?"

There was a small pause. "Can't make it. I've got something on. Say hallo for me." Kevin heard the disappointment in his last sentence.

"I will. See you on Monday."

"Bye, Kevin."

That went better. He knew it would. He could hide behind the banter. One could spar with Al. Nothing went deep and no one got cut. Nice and light. Of course Al could dish it out as well as any of them. Being black he had to be doubly sharp.

"Hey, Kev, why do coloureds wear baggy trousers?" said Chris, stripping more tape for the masking paper, the spray gun at his feet.

"Tell me," said Kevin. Al couldn't help listening.

"Because their knee grows."

"Ha, ha, Chris," said Al. "Was that the end of playtime bell just now?"

When Kevin thought about it he knew very little about Al. What did he do at the weekend?

Kevin dialled Chris's number. It rang three times and he thought of hanging up. He could say he tried. Four times. Five. Six. That's enough. Seven. Eight -

"Yeah."

"Chris?" he managed. He'd so convinced himself that no one was going to answer he was taken aback.

"Kev. How's tricks?"

"Okay. Listen -"

"Have I a choice?"

"You could hang up. Are you going to listen or what?"

"I'm all ears. But are you okay? You don't sound your usual witty self. And I mean witty beginning with an es and aitch. You -"

"Kurt's here."

"The frog?"

"Yep. The frog. Kermit. Pig-dog." This was good. He sounded like himself. The tone of his voice was his. Not some strangled impersonation of him.

"At your place?"

"No. The usual for lunch. He said he'd be there at midday."

"That's less than an hour."

"Can you make it?" The conversation was going on too long. So he lied. "I've got to phone Mick now."

"Not for twelve. How long are you staying for?"

Kevin felt his blood suddenly boil. He wanted to shout back that he had no idea. "I don't know. He's flying back this evening. He'll have to catch the train. I don't know. Can you make it?"

"I'll try."

"Okay. See you."

"Kev -" But he had replaced the receiver before he could hear more. He stood over the phone thinking of Chris doing the same at the other end. Don't ring, he willed. Moments ticked by.

He hoped Chris wouldn't be able to make it. He was never completely at ease with him.

The phone had rung. He strode across the room and stood over it, letting it ring a further two times before picking it up. "Hospital. Maternity ward."

"Hey, what?" she said. Then more composed: "Sorry I -"

"It's okay, it's me," he sniggered.

"Kevin, you arse." He felt her smile, but he couldn't see her. He only had one image of Sandra in his mind.

"You know me better than I thought." He heard her laugh. Her joy spurred his familiarity. "And you still want to get together?"

"I'll give you a second chance."

"Thanks for your kindness and generosity."

"Yours sincerely," she said.

"Yeah, right." But he only later understood the reference to signing off a letter. "What do you want to do? Disco? Dinner? Cinema? Cock-fighting?"

"What? Do they do cock-fights here?"

"Not the kind you're thinking of."

"You're wicked."

"I hope you are too."

"I'm having second thoughts about you."

"Dinner? Cinema?"

"Both?"

"You're on."

They made their arrangements before signing off.

"Yes," he said, clenching his fist and jerking his elbow with victory.

He'd chatted her up outside the women's toilets at the pub. She'd been waiting to go in.

"Busy tonight," he smiled going into the men's. When he came out she was still waiting. "The men's are free."

"I'll wait," she smiled.

"Mind if I wait with you?" he said. She blushed, but quickly recovered. "Kevin," he said holding out his hand.

"Sandra." And she took his hand.

"Cold hands," he remarked.

"Warm heart."

They heard the toilet latch being pulled back. Almost simultaneously another girl appeared from the pub.

"You want to give me a ring some time?" he said.

"What for?"

"I like the one on your little finger there."

She laughed.

"You waiting?" asked the newcomer, letting the girl from the toilet pass.

"Yeah," said Sandra. "You're a fresh one," she said to Kevin.

"You ain't heard nothing, yet."

She rifled her handbag and gave Kevin a small notepad and pen. "See you in a minute," she said.

"Yeah, I've got to wash my hands," he said.

She shrieked. The newcomer was not amused, but Kevin still grinned at her.

After giving Sandra her notepad and pen Kevin returned to his pals. Sandra went to her group. Whenever possible they exchanged a glance and a smile.

The following evening he went out. Had she phoned and complained that he wasn't in she would have dropped a notch in his estimation. But he judged her correctly. She'd left it a day before phoning. She was cool.

Touch my mind

Touch my mind
Leave your hate behind

Touch my mind
My love may unwind

Such is my mind
Hide what you find

Much as I mind
My love may blind

Clutch my mind
My love may bind

Be so kind
As to touch my mind

Chris wasn't going to phone back.

He thought of giving Mick another try, but decided against it.

He had about thirty minutes to kill before leaving. The thought of drinking a pint made him feel nauseous.

Kevin decided he should eat something before going. But the thought of eating made him uneasy.

He went to the kitchen and dropped a slice of bread in the toaster.

"What do you think?" asked Kevin.

"I agree," said Kurt. "It's the best place so far."

It was far from the small hole in the wall discotheque they were used to. This was a big dance hall from a bygone era. Their reasoning was that it would have more choice.

"Okay, let's eat."

The lads, for that was what they were, walked along the promenade, the sea air whipping their hair about.

"If that's it, I'll give you the money for a haircut, son."

"It's fashionable, Dad."

"To look like a girl?"

"Yes."

"I'll ask your mother whether she can dig out some old dresses for you, then."

Kurt and Kevin ate, went back as late as possible to the guest house to get showered and changed and were at the dance hall early enough to get in unhindered. By nine it was filling up nicely. With lads. There were clusters of girls. There were couples. But more than anything else there were lads.

"Come on, let's do a round," said Kevin.

"We've only just sat down," said Kurt.

"We've got to be fast."

"I'm getting dizzy going round and round."

"Do you want others to get the talent?"

"Okay, okay. I'm up. Let's go. But not so fast. I don't want to spill my pint."

Kevin ate the toast dry. He sat at the dining table eating it.

The silence was overwhelming. And he felt as alone as David in the clinically white room in Kubrick's *2001 a space odyssey*.

He took small bites of the toast. It taste burnt and bland in his mouth. He didn't really chew. Instead he soaked each piece in saliva and pulped it with his tongue. Only before swallowing did he mash it with his teeth.

He should put on some music.

As bland as the toast were the pepper and saltcellars sitting on the table. They were the spoils of his petty theft at some stuck-up wine-bar. Drunken fool.

Sandra had asked him about his stealing. He'd replied: "It's instinctual. A man's thing. You know, hunter-gatherer. That's the gatherer in me."

He was warmed when she said: "Yes, well, your hunting's over."

He continued to ignore the writing paper and the pen.

On the wall was a copy of Claude Monet's *Parliament in London*. It was a foggy picture, predominantly blue, parliament silhouetted behind the Thames with the fire of a low sun. He'd picked it up in a market on their Corfu holiday. There had been so many of these types of paintings. The area had looked like a colourful collection from a painting-by-numbers competition. He wasn't sure why he bought it. Sandra had liked one of people, mainly women with parasols at a riverside, a Georges Seurat. He thought it fine, but he didn't want to buy something she liked for his flat. He favoured some skulls by Paul Cézanne. He knew she would hate them and didn't ask her opinion. Then there was Munch's *The Scream*. But it was gaudy and too disturbing. Finally he bought the Monet.

The Greek at the stall had been a character. He had told them the artists and then reeled off galleries as if he'd regularly visited them: Guggenheim, Louvre, Tate. They had nodded knowingly. And he went further, insisting that his paintings were as good. No. They were sometimes better, because they were bright and fresh.

And so they looked in that wonderful Mediterranean light, every colour elevated to a distinctly primary one.

Kevin looked at the painting. The paint was lumpy and could not be framed behind glass. Dust had settled in the rills and small ridges.

The painting meant nothing to him. He should have bought the skulls. Their appeal would have worn off too. Of course Sandra's choice would have been classy and lasting. But the painting would have been another piece of her invading his life when she was supposed to be leaving.

Kevin surveyed the room and came to realise that a lot of things meant little to him. Oh, they possessed significance, if only because they evoked, even provoked, some memory. But they seemed to have become detached from his memory. He saw everything anew. The things in his flat hadn't changed, but his way of regarding them had.

Even the cheeky corkscrew, which had produced a cockeyed smile on Sandra's face, was just a piece of metal. For him, buying it was a highlight of an otherwise harrowing beach holiday. Of course, every memory of Sandra had become precious. But the things that reminded him of her, the things themselves, had become arbitrary.

There was an awful sense of everything becoming arbitrary.

"Stop faffing around," he said aloud and stuffed the last bit of toast in his mouth and chewed aggressively. He gulped down the remains of his lukewarm coffee.

He got up, the chair scraping the floor, and took his plate to the bowl in the kitchen sink.

Then he went to the bedroom and searched for a T-shirt. At first he couldn't find anything suitable. Eventually he found his plain dark blue one with the tiny white dolphins springing on each sleeve. It was a present from his sister Maggie, from a Christmas or three ago. The colours were still relatively bright and the shirt certainly wasn't worn enough to be relegated to his work stack: those worn underneath his overall.

That Christmas was the first time they weren't all together. Rosie and Gary had been absent. Gary had spent Christmas day at his in-laws and Rosie was somewhere abroad with her boyfriend.

The presents had grown up with them. Little Rosie had once saved her pocket money to buy him a tin of salted peanuts and a Frey Bentos steak and kidney pie.

Kevin remembered his childhood Christmases primarily as a times of roast turkey and roast backs. There was only one gas-fire in the lounge where their presents were heaped under the tree. Being Christmas they tried to be nice to each other and took turns sitting closer to the fire. Those further away were cold in their pyjamas and those close to the fire had to continually shift their roasting backs. Eventually the room was warm enough and everyone was happy.

He also remembered it as a time of feeling painfully full and having a buzzing headache from too much food and too much television. The telly wasn't rationed that day. Food neither. But after the midday coming on three o'clock - then after the Queen's speech - turkey lunch with stuffing and cranberry jelly, carrots, sprouts and roast potatoes, there were turkey sandwiches in the evening, and the next day. And, as if they hadn't had enough turkey, their father always boiled up the bones to make his awful turkey soup.

He still didn't have to leave for another ten minutes, but he now wanted to get out.

At the full-length mirror by the door he checked himself.

"Whoa," he said. "It's like a bleedin' ice-rink here." He had slipped and almost fallen.

He'd told Sandra about using her hair spray over the polished floorboards. "You want me to look good, don't you?" she called from the bathroom.

"Well, I won't look good with a bloody nose."

After combing his hair he checked he had his car keys. "Are you ready?"

"Yes, on my way."

He knew better than to open the flat door. Sandra's "on my way" was code for at least "another ten minutes."

Kevin tried to smile in the mirror, but his image betrayed him and he had to look away.

"Your father's not vain," said his Mum. "He just finds the mirrors distressing." A blanket was draped over the bedroom dressing table mirror.

"I'm sorry," said his Dad.

"Don't be silly," said Kevin.

His father hung heavily onto his shoulder. He was now a bag of bones. But he was still in pain. He'd come off chemotherapy and he'd stopped eating. There was no point, he said. Water was all he took.

Struggling with him to the toilet confronted Kevin with the brunt of his father's deterioration.

His father could barely stand, his pyjamas miraculously hanging from him, but he insisted on undressing and sitting alone. Just as, weeks ago, he wanted to walk unaided across the hospital car park. He staggered, his movement awkward as if he were learning to walk on stilts. And way back then his legs had indeed resembled sticks.

Kevin virtually fled the apartment.

Out on the street was familiarity and strangeness. He recognised everything. Everything was in its place. The world was at it should be. And yet, it was as if he was seeing his surroundings for the first time. Things he'd taken for granted asserted themselves.

He saw the flaking brown paint of the front garden fence, the chimneys of the houses opposite looking like straight flower pots, the broken gutter of number sixteen, the cat-shaped doorbell of number twenty, the beware of the dog sign at number twenty-two, the -

Of course if she'd stayed with him, she wouldn't have been at the crossroads on the high street on Wednesday night. They would have been together if they'd had the kid. But who was he kidding? If they hadn't broken up then, then they would have broken up later. And with a kid in tow it would have been worse. Really horrible.

He needed to change his frame of mind. But guilt swamped him. He couldn't simply forget Sandra. Have a beer and a laugh. It'll all be okay.

The very thought of beer made him feel sick.

Normally he strode, but now he walked as if he didn't really want to arrive.

He contemplated returning to the flat. The solitude was inviting, but the flat itself wasn't.

Kevin decided that he wouldn't tell them in the pub. He wasn't sure he could get away with it. But he steeled himself nonetheless.

He hadn't seen Kurt for a couple of years.

"What do you think?" said Kevin.

"You take the blonde," said Kurt.

"Okay. I like blondes."

"Yeah?"

"Yeah. They get dirty quicker. Drink up, let's go."

The situation in the dance hall had been growing decidedly desperate. Where were all the Scandinavian girls Kurt had read about? This seaside resort was supposed to be besieged by them. The two girls talking to one another appeared to be the only decent ones free. Normally when they came as a pair, one was a gargoyle. Kevin saw clusters of men in their vicinity. He imagined them getting their mum together to make a move.

"Look how much I've got," said Kurt holding up his half filled pint. "They are not going anywhere."

"That's what you think. Put it down and let's go."

"But Kev -"

Kevin strode towards the girls his smile broadening as he approached.

"You look as if you're in need of a dance," he said, relieved to see Kurt at his side.

There was that moment of hesitation in the girls as they sized up the boys. They didn't really have time to exchange looks.

The dark-haired one accepted first. Kevin knew that Kurt had bagged the stronger personality. He also realised that he'd got the tastier one to boot. His own wasn't a gargoyle, or a looker, but she had great jugs.

They spent the evening together. The boys were proud that they'd picked up the girls against all odds. Just before closing time they left. It was too dark and cold for a beach walk. So they stayed on the road, popping into the brightness of an arcade if it was open.

Eventually they came to a crossroads. As couples they stood some distance apart, Kevin at a wall with his blonde, Kurt near a lamppost with his girl, necking, cuddling, talking thickly and whispering naughty words. Kevin signalled to Kurt that his girl was willing to come back to the hotel room.

Then Kevin was at the main-road. Even on a Sunday it was terribly busy. He crossed to the island and waited for a gap in the traffic.

He saw a lad who looked like Chris in a patterned woollen bomber jacket. But it wasn't him. Kevin had possessed just such a jacket for about two hours.

"It's okay with Mum," Kevin pleaded.

"I don't care," his Dad said. "I gave you money to buy a winter coat."

"But it's really warm. Look, it's fleeced inside."

"It's a bum freezer. Take it back and get a long winter coat."

So to protect his bum against possible frostbite he bought a long trench coat, as heavy as a blanket, black as night.

"Black suits you," said Sandra.

He'd wear black on Wednesday and she wouldn't see him.

Yeah and he'd worn a black polo-neck sweater to the small family circus.

"She didn't suffer," said Tim. "It was instant."

And a person's life had changed under the big top too. In an instant.

"I love the circus," said Sandra.

"I haven't been since I was a kid," said Kevin.

They had been the only childless couple amongst the hordes of restless children and reserved adults.

The last act was a fire-eater. He was a young lad, also in black. Sandra said he was a dish.

He routinely ate fire, rotated lit rods, putting out the flames with his mouth, lighting other ends from his mouth. Then he went on to blowing fire into the air. The heat was tremendous. His finale was to turn whilst blowing fire into the air to create a twister of fire. Unfortunately patches of his face caught fire. For a moment he didn't notice. Such was the heat. Then he fled, clutching his face, falling at the edge of the ring, burying his face in his hands, hunched on the ground. The shock was so complete that no one in the audience screamed or cried out. The fire-eater himself didn't make a noise. His mouth was probably still full of spirit. He was taken off and others came on and tried to entertain. Kevin thought the guy would return for the end applause to show that he was okay. But he didn't.

He'd undoubtedly been rushed to hospital. Not only were his good looks probably ruined; he could also be out of a job. Who'd employ a fire-eater with a burnt face? His life had changed in an instant.

Kevin turned left at the T-junction and went over the bridge. He crossed the road before reaching the fire station.

He knew he needed to change his frame of mind.

"Kurt," said Mick, "could you take the mini back in your lunchtime? Kevin, you could follow."

Mick's garage was a family business in that he ran it and his family used it. Every couple of months or so his mother's mini was in for a servicing and a clean. It was her pride and joy. More so since she'd won a sunroof on some phone-in radio competition.

Kurt had spent a good part of the morning polishing and waxing. He'd paid special attention to the leather upholstery.

"You could pop into the chippie on the way back," said Mick. "I'll get lunch." He shouted into the garage that lunch was on him and that they should place their orders with Kurt and Kevin.

Kevin followed Kurt in his car until the hazard warning lights of the mini went on and Kurt pulled over. Kevin did the same. A car hooted at the unexpected manoeuvre, but Kevin ignored it as he got out and hurried to mini. Kurt didn't move. He just sat there.

Kevin was about to say something when he saw it. Kurt had opened the sunroof. It was the right day for it. But all down his left arm and splashed on the passenger seat was dirty white bird shit. Kevin doubled over with laughter.

He was nearing the pub.

A car passed by. Its windows were down and the music blaring. He recognised the snippet as the current number one: Wham! *Wake me up before you go go*. Sandra would have heard it before it became number one. Yes, she would have liked it. He knew. But now she was gone and it didn't matter. Nothing mattered. For she'd never hear next week's hit. She'd never know tomorrow's blockbuster. Nothing mattered. It was only entertainment. And then did anything really matter? All those classroom lessons, all that knowledge, all that learning, all those tears, ... What had it brought her?

He could hear his own voice saying that she would live on in him. The memory of her would live on. But now, right now, as he walked along this bland street, he could not fully picture her. He tried to imagine her face, but all he got were pieces, pieces that shifted and faded, never allowing him a full picture.

Kevin knew he was losing it. This is madness, he said to himself. And what was he doing out here going to a pub? He wasn't up to the meeting. Could he turn around? He was almost there. And would he tell them about Sandra? He wasn't sure. No. He didn't want to tell them. But would he? He wasn't sure he could hold it in.

He could handle Steve and Kurt. But he wasn't sure about Chris. If Chris turned up he could be in trouble. Chris was merciless, razor sharp.

"I thought you were a working class hero," said Chris, "but you're something far worse: you're a social climber." Maybe Tony had said something to him? Tony had bumped into him when he was with Helen. She and Tony had been fine, but Kevin had squirmed with the awkwardness of the situation. What a mess.

He took a deep breath before entering the pub.

He saw them immediately. Kurt and Steve were sitting alongside each other on the cushioned bench that ran the wall. At the small round table in front of them were three empty chairs. No Chris. Good.

"This great steaming turd on his chest," Steve was saying.

Kurt's mouth dropped before he laughed.

Kevin smiled as he approached.

"It wasn't steaming," said Kevin, nodding at Steve and shaking Kurt's hand.

"Hey, Kev," said Kurt, still laughing.

"Does it matter?" said Steve.

"You want anything?" asked Kevin, jerking his head towards the bar.

Kurt shook his head.

"I'm all right," said Steve.

Kevin went over to the bar. They'd not noticed anything and he was pleased.

It was Terry's day off. The old boot was behind the bar.

"Usual Kev?" she asked.

"Yeah, Tina. Thanks."

He watched her fetch a sleever from the shelf above the bar.

Tina was a tough old boot. She was probably not yet thirty, but she was as leathery as a fifty year old. Kevin and the boys reckoned she'd worked her way through most of the clientele. She took any willing, or probably unknowing, stragglers at the end of the evening. Only Chris admitted to her giving him head. Otherwise the lads stuck together and hadn't fallen prey to her. Safety in numbers. She frightened Kevin. She was awesome.

She was a stalking lioness on a David Attenborough programme waiting to pounce on a stray or incapacitated gazelle.

He was climbing over his bigger brother Gary. As boys they wrestled, fighting like lion cubs and the girls and Mum liked to watch wrestling on television late Saturday afternoon. The boys watched too, but they scorned and scoffed and said it was fixed. They preferred watching the boxing with their Dad. "I'll box your ears, Kevin, if I catch you doing that again."

He looked about as she pulled the pint. The place was half empty. But it was early. By one o'clock it would be full. The menu was bog standard but the quality not bad. He should eat something. One slice of dry toast was not enough. The glass cabinet sitting at the end of the bar contained an assortment of baguettes in cling film. There were some muffins too.

He pulled his small wad of notes out of his back pocket. When he could avoid it he didn't carry a wallet, especially when he wasn't wearing a jacket. A wallet bulged his jeans back pocket and made sitting uncomfortable. Bum bags were for ponces. He liked to carry cash. He wasn't a credit card fan and called them debit cards, anyway. Mick gave them their pay in packets at the end of each month. The money came in small stapled-closed manila envelopes with a pattern of holes so you could see the coins. The staple went through a corner of the notes, so you could check them too. Mick went round handing them out like Father Christmas handing out gifts. Yes, with hard cash you knew where you were.

"What baguettes have you got?" he asked as Tina placed the pint in front of him.

"Ham and egg, cheese and tomato, cheese and onion, chicken and - "

"Cheese and tomato."

There never seemed to be enough food during his childhood. The choice was there: they could have one orange or one apple or one banana for supper. But Kevin was often quite hungry. One of his earliest memories as a three or four year old was linked to hunger. In the night he had sneaked to the kitchen where his mother had prepared a bowl of onions for a stew the next day. Despite burning eyes he ate as many as he could. Later, in the night, his mother was at his bedside trying to comfort him, but other than drinking gallons of water there was nothing to quell his pain and stop his groaning.

He sipped the top off his pint. The taste made him feel lousy.

Kevin paid up and took his pint and baguette to the table. He sat with the door and half of the room in front of him.

"Okay Kev?" asked Steve.

Had they noticed something? "Yeah, why not?"

"Anybody else coming?" asked Kurt.

"Chris said he'd try to make it. Otherwise this is it."

Kurt nodded. And they were silent for a moment. Kevin spoke first. "So how're you doing, you old sour Kraut?"

"Probably better than you."

"What do you mean?" Again he wondered whether they had noticed something and concentrated on unwrapping his baguette.

"It is as depressing as ever here. IRA bombings. The miners' strike. Your Iron Lady has a strangle hold on the country."

"It's still rosy in Hamburg, then," said Kevin.

"Germany is booming."

"It's not so bad here," said Steve.

"No?" asked Kevin. And they laughed.

"Actually, you don't look too well, Kevin," said Kurt.

"Yeah, you look as if you've seen a ghost," Steve added.

Should he tell them?

"Just tired lads," he said. "That's all."

"Come on, Kurt," said Steve, "tell us about skiing, then."

"Yes, I will. But tell me Kevin, is this story about Jim true?"

"Of course, it's true," said Steve.

"Same as Steve, I heard it yesterday." He took a big bite out of his baguette.

"Yes, but is it true?"

"I don't know," Kevin said around his mouthful. "We'll have to get it from the horse's mouth."

"It doesn't matter, I suppose," said Kurt. He took a gulp of his pint. Steve did the same.

"I went skiing at Christmas," Kurt began. "I'm not saying it to show off," he added quickly. "But something happened that fits with what happened to Jim."

Kevin raised is eyebrows. He was still chewing. It was like eating rubber. There was too much dough and cheese. Not enough tomato. Stodge.

"Everyone skis in Germany. Not in Hamburg, of course. Austria. We were a group of couples. I went with my girlfriend."

"You've got a *Fräulein*?" asked Kevin, around the remains of his mouthful.

"Yes. And she does not have a white stick."

Kevin took a welcome sip of his pint as Kurt continued. He was grateful for the liquid but not its taste.

"We were three couples. I was the only one in ski school. On the second day there was a woman who suddenly had the urge to go. The instructor just wanted to get on. He was frustrated with us. I think it was his first time teaching absolute beginners..."

Andrea had sent him a postcard from a skiing trip. Actually it wasn't a postcard but a photograph of her in the full outfit. Clear blue sky was behind her, as if she was at the top of a mountain; perhaps she was. And her expression said she was on top of the world. She'd stuck a stamp on the back and written something he'd forgotten. The only phrase he attached to her was: "If you don't like something, change it." The card seemed to reinforce the way she looked at life. He had it somewhere. It was the only photograph he had of her.

"...He told her to go behind a hill," Kurt was saying. "There were no toilets up there. She wasn't too happy. I mean, she was about forty, I suppose. Anyway, she disappeared and he went on telling us something. And whilst he's talking she slid out from behind the hill. She was crouched with her salopettes around her ankles. But -"

"Mooning?" said Steve excitedly.

"Yes. But on the end of one of her skis was a steaming turd."

"I don't believe it," laughed Steve.

"I was there," said Kurt.

Kevin smiled. "What happened?"

"She carried on down to the village. She never came back. We never saw her again."

"This is a joke," said Kevin.

"I was there."

"Pull the other one," said Steve. "It's got bells on it."

"They're always steaming, aren't they?" said Kevin.

"It's cold up there, you know. Don't believe me, if you don't want to. But I was there."

Kevin tore off another bite from his baguette. He was beginning to wonder whether he could finish it.

More people were entering the pub and it was filling up nicely.

A girl carrying a tray approached them. "Steak and kidney pie?"

Kurt raised his hand. "That's me."

"But you can call him Kurt," said Steve.

Kevin groaned and the girl from the kitchen gave a weary smile.

The plate of food, which had dollop of mushy peas and a generous portion of country chips, was placed in front of Kurt.

"So, you were visiting your Mum, then?" said Kevin as casually as possible.

Kurt's mother and father were divorced. Kurt had left Mick's to work at his German father's garage in Hamburg. The money and, of course, the prospects were too good for him to pass up. At Mick's he'd been relatively new and therefore at the bottom of the food chain. But he'd gained a lot of valuable experience.

"It was her birthday on Friday. So I surprised her."

"And us," said Steve.

"Why aren't you with her now?"

"A friend bought her tickets for a show I'm too embarrassed to mention."

"Come on," said Kevin.

"California dream boys?" said Steve.

"I'm not saying."

There was a silence.

"When's your plane?"

"Seven o'clock. To be safe I want to get the three o'clock train."

He was sitting opposite Kurt on the train. It had been a long and eventful day. The girls had not come back to the hotel that night. Kurt's sensible one had gone on about her worrying aunt. And as they lay in bed, excited at the prospect of meeting them the following day, Kurt spoke out of the darkness.

"But we can't bring them back here. We have to check out by eleven."

"Well done, Sherlock," said Kevin.

"What are we going to do?" They had arranged to meet the girls at the cinema at eleven in the morning. Ken Russell's film of The Who's *Tommy* was playing.

"I'll talk to the landlord in the morning. Maybe we can get an extension."

"If he says yes, he will want money."

"Yeah. Well the skinflint's not getting another penny out of me for this dump."

Kevin was true to his word. The skinflint didn't get another penny out them. But they didn't keep the room either.

They met the girl's, watched the film between snogs, had lunch, wandered the promenade and arcades, the uncompromising light of the day revealing weatherworn colours, flaking paint. And then they were saying goodbye, exchanging phone numbers and addresses and making promises that were never kept.

"We didn't do too bad," said Kevin, above the noise of the train.

"No, we picked up the only two decent birds in the place."

"Where did you read about all those Scandinavian girls?" Kurt answered.

"News of the Screws," exclaimed Kevin. "You can't believe that rag." Kevin should have checked. Kurt wasn't born here. He came over when he was quite young. Oh, he was a great guy, but he wasn't street-wise. He was a foreigner doing a damned good impression of an Englishman. You couldn't fault his accent. But sometimes his naïvety gave the game away.

They were both weary. It had been a long Saturday night, Sunday morning. And they'd been up early on Sunday to shower and get ready. All that fresh air had taken its toll too. Kevin was slightly delirious.

"What's it all about, Alfie?" he asked, idly.

"Life?" said Kurt, taking him seriously.

"Yeah, why not?"

"I would say finding significance."

"What?" said Kevin, startled.

"Everyone has to feel significant."

"Oh, Kurt that's too heavy for me. You read that on the back of a matchbox, or what? I'm tired. I'm going to get some shut-eye."

"You miss anything here?" asked Steve, putting down his pint.

"The humour?" asked Kevin.

"We have a laugh over there too. The humour is just different."

"Don't mention the War," said Steve in a stage whisper. But it was a cheap shot that had been done to death with Kurt.

"You gonad," said Kevin.

Kurt was silent and Steve grew awkward.

There was a while when Kurt had suffered a morning greeting of Heil Hitler. Until Mick put a stop to it. Some occasionally referred to him as the Nazi, but never to his face. All this was swept aside when he became Kurt the frog.

"More than anything," Kurt began, "I miss the treasure hunts."

Kevin felt Steve's relief. He was relieved himself. Yes, a joke was a joke, but Kevin had been over to Germany. The young people were as alive and vibrant as here. And in Hamburg Kevin was given an open-armed welcome. Of course, there was much talk of The Beatles and music and how quirky, sometimes quaint Britain was. They made his home country sound exciting. So much so that he had found himself trying to find fault, in some way, to balance things out. He even went so far as to counter by making positive statements about what he'd seen in Germany. He spoke of cleanliness and order, the punctuality of the buses and trains: down to the minute, he said.

"And the frog costume?" said Kevin. And as if they had rehearsed he and Steve began croaking.

Kurt laughed.

Kevin and Steve laughed too. But Kevin stopped before it became forced or uncontrollable. Grief took him and he looked into his pint. Then he took a chunk out of his roll. And his mouthful camouflaged his twisted smile.

"I still think it was a good idea," said Kurt.

Mick and his wife organised an annual treasure hunt. It was known as the Black Toad Treasure Hunt, on account of Mick's Humber Pullman. Called the black toad it was his pride and joy. Mick's wife's colleagues from the bakery and Mick's lads participated. The bakers themselves were fine, but there were namby-pamby office types too. Kevin and co. made a sport out of having a go at them. The start of the hunt was always at some car park. There each team was handed a sheet of directions, clues to look for, puzzles to solve and things to collect for their treasure-trove. Mick and his wife would drive about for a while, but otherwise the teams were left to their own devices. Kevin and the others were the baddies. They were the Dick Dastardly and Muttley of *Wacky Races*. They always came well equipped with compass, string, paint, all manner of bric-a-brac, notes and coins of all denominations. But unlike the *Wacky Races* team they nearly always won. Once or twice they came second. And of course they cheated and lied. Wherever possible they left false clues. On one occasion they posted official-looking signs: Black Toad Treasure Hunt this way. And some of the cars behind them fell for it. The bizarre thing was, was that they still solved some clues.

As a joke Martin had suggested telling Kurt that this year's treasure hunt was to be in fancy dress. It was surprisingly easy to convince him. They took him one lunchtime for a fitting, saying that they'd tried on their costumes and ordered them already. When he pulled back the curtain of the changing cubicle he asked them to button him up at the back. "Going to the toilet is going to be a problem," he said, his voice muffled by the outsized frog's head. They could barely contain themselves. And even when they all took photographs, one of which would have pride of place on the pin board amongst the holiday postcards, he still didn't realise he'd been had. For days afterwards, even now, he thought it was a good idea. He even wanted them to do it just for a laugh.

For many a morning he was greeted by a chorus of croaking.

"We had a corker this year," said Kevin.

"And?"

"We won," he said.

"I didn't expect anything less."

Kevin wanted to elaborate but nothing came to mind.

"You miss anything else?" asked Steve. He had been silent. He knew of the treasure hunts. They were legendary. But they were employee-only affairs.

"The beer?"

"Germany is strong on beer and football, too."

"That's not beer," said Steve. "That's lager."

"It's not."

"It's not real ale, that's for sure."

"Headless and lukewarm," smiled Kurt.

"Hey, Chris," said Steve suddenly.

Kevin looked round.

Chris greeted Kurt first. They shook hands and slagged one another off, Chris getting the upper hand.

"I'm skint lads, so you won't mind if I get myself one," he said, placing his packet of cigarettes, his car keys on top, on the table. Kevin had been in his car once. It was an ashtray on wheels.

"Get me half a shandy and you can have this," said Kevin.

Chris looked at him suspiciously.

"I'm not feeling too hot."

Chris looked at the others for confirmation that this was Kevin before him.

"I've hardly touched it." Kevin looked at Kurt. "I'll give Kurt a lift to the station."

"I can walk," said Kurt. "The bag's not heavy."

"I'll give you a lift."

Kurt nodded his thanks.

"Okay," said Chris. "Half a shandy coming up."

He left to the bar.

Kevin felt uneasy. Chris's presence would mean cranking up his guard a number of notches. If they were soldiers then Steve and Kurt would be the grunts, Chris and Kevin would be the sergeants.

"He hasn't changed," said Kurt.

"A leotard never changes its spots," said Steve.

Kurt smiled.

Kevin pushed the pint over to the spare place and took another bite out of his roll. He'd hit the half way mark.

Chris returned and put the half pint in front of Kevin. "There we are madam." Kevin nodded. His mouth was full. Chris sat down and raised the pint. "Cheers," he said. The others followed suit. Kevin pointed to his chewing mouth.

As Chris took his first gulp Steve said: "Kev topped it up in the loo."

Chris sprayed the beer uncontrollably, but then directed the last of it in Kevin's direction.

Steve and Kurt laughed, but Kevin, pushing his chair backwards, scraping the floor with a horrible screech, was on his feet. Chris had realised the joke and was wiping his mouth on Kurt's serviette. Kevin couldn't hide his anger. "Steve, you fucking idiot," a gob of dough flying from his mouth onto the table.

Steve and Kurt were horrified. Chris regarded him strangely too.

"Okay, boys," said the old boot, loudly.

The others looked over at her and Kevin scrambled to think of something to get himself off the hook.

Kevin smiled, taking Kurt's crumpled serviette Chris had thrown down and plucking the gob of food from the table. "You could have waited until I was out of range. I'm soaked." But he wasn't soaked.

"You didn't get as much as me," said Kurt.

Chris put the pint to his lips again. "If Kev can piss this, then, ladies and gentlemen, we are looking at the next millionaire."

"I'll tell you something though, Kev," said Chris. "You don't look too good."

"It's been two heavy nights in a row."

"I would have said too much choking the bishop."

"What?" said Kurt, shaking his head and looking for an explanation.

"Don't think person," said Steve. "Think of the chess piece." A slow smile appeared on Kurt's face, although Kevin still wondered whether he had understood.

"Two heavy nights and one altercation," said Chris.

"Altercation," said Steve in a hoity-toity voice. "How very sanguine."

"You look at my woman again I'll put you in an oxygen tent!" threatened the stranger.

Kevin felt under attack and defenceless. He struggled to maintain his composure. He had little control over his expression. Like those nancy French balls of old where they held masks on sticks in front of their eyes Kevin too had a selection of masks. They were the different faces he presented to different people. He thought he'd left the house with his full complement, but now he saw that most were waterlogged and useless.

He wasn't going to last a continual onslaught.

"What happened?" asked Kurt.

"Some guy's woman saw the light of day," Chris said. "And he didn't like it."

Kurt was confused, but Kevin remained silent and Steve stepped in. Whilst he explained the tussle with guy who challenged Kevin because of the looks he had exchanged with his girlfriend Kevin ate.

"And Kevin said," Steve went on. "You'll look funny picking up your teeth with a broken arm."

Did he say that? Kevin wondered. He didn't remember saying it.

"The girl said: stop it. But Kev and this guy were doing a face-off. Like boxers do before a fight. This guy made the first move. He shoved Kev. Didn't he?" Kevin didn't answer. "And Kev fell onto a table. Terry heard the glasses going over and shouted something. There were so many people standing about, he probably hadn't seen the face-off."

"Then what?" asked Kurt, hoping Kevin would continue.

And Steve went on to tell how Kevin had got up and began another face-off as if nothing had happened. Kev had nutted the guy and kneed him in the crotch. As he went down Kevin finished him with a kick. Terry gave them both a bollocking and chucked them out.

Kurt appeared enthralled and Kevin wondered whether life in Germany was more pedestrian.

Weapons at the ready they made their way between the cars.

Before they reached him the man got up. He looked scared. "Okay lads, what are you doing?" On seeing his uniform they tried to conceal their weapons.

"This is my garage," said Mick.

"You're the owner?"

"Yes."

The officer relaxed and walked towards them. Kevin knew he must have been watching them and wondering what to do. Mick leant his outsized spanner against the door. The officer was impressed. Mick got out his wallet and showed him his business card.

The officer nodded and then spoke into his walkie-talkie. It sounded as if he was cancelling some backup he'd requested. After all there were four of them and they looked intimidating.

"My partner is patrolling," he said. "Another car is on the way. Shall we all go inside and see what's missing?" He wanted to keep them together.

Mick nodded and they went in. The officer stayed near the door and talked into his walkie-talkie whilst they wandered about.

At first everything looked undisturbed.

Mick went up to his office. After a while the officer joined him.

Then Martin shouted that a power drill was missing.

To the untrained eye the place looked a mess. But everything had its place and was tidied away at the end of the working day. It was also a good way of minimising petty theft.

Mick and the policeman were still in the office when Kurt gestured Martin and Kevin over. He spoke quietly and hurriedly. "When I was on my way to Johnson's, I saw two blacks going passed the tile factory. They were carrying a holdall between them."

"So it was heavy," said Kevin.

"Come here, lads," Mick called from the office.

Because the officer was on the other side of Mick's desk the three of them could only gather at the entrance.

"What's the damage?"

Martin spoke for them. "The power drill, the blow-lamp, the spray gun and the new toolbox." The officer scribbled in his notebook.

"Could we talk to you alone?" asked Martin.

Mick looked at the officer.

"No problem," he said, snapping his notebook shut and leaving them.

"Go and take a look," said Mick, when Kurt had told him what he'd seen. "I have to stay here. Don't take any risks."

They left the office and strode across the garage.

"You're not off to do anything silly now," said the officer walking to cut them off at the garage door.

"They're just going to take a look around," Mick called.

"You want to leave those pieces here?" It wasn't a question.

Mick nodded and they put their metal on a workbench.

Once out of the yard they ran back passed Johnson's and piled into Kurt's car. At the lights not a soul was in sight and they went through red. They drove up a side road and there, way ahead of them, on the crest of the hill, they saw two figures lugging a heavy bag.

"Yes, I heard about it," said Chris, answering Kurt's question about Jim's bedroom antics. "I tell you that guy has so many women he can't change the bedding fast enough. His sheets crackle when he lies down." Kurt gave him a queer look. "The sheets are that crispy."

"Urh," said Kurt delightedly.

"Snap, crackle and pop," said Steve.

Kevin made a mental note to change his own sheets. He didn't do it regularly, only when it occurred to him.

Kurt went on to retelling his skiing story and Kevin watched him. Kurt was a good guy. He was genuine, a little naïve, but one of the good guys. He visited his mother.

"Take care of your mother," his father said. Of course they'd take care of her. It didn't need saying. Don't insult us, Dad. What kind of sons do you think we are? And his father added: "Don't cry boys." And The Cure were forever singing that *boys don't cry*. "This is not how I want to remember you." But he was dying, so he wouldn't remember anything, would he? Who knows? It was a terrible thought.

He was about to think about Sandra, wondering why he was thinking so much about his Dad, when he heard his name.

"That's right, isn't it, Kev?" said Chris.

"What? I was miles away."

"Earth to Kevin," said Kurt good-humouredly.

"I was telling Kurt about Snotridge." Notridge was a new guy at the garage. He seemed to have a perpetual cold. "He leaves goo all over the tools."

"Yeah," said Kevin happy to contribute with a cheap shot. "It's like the saliva from Alien." And he lifted his hand off the table as if it were covered in some viscous dripping substance.

"He's a bloody hooligan. On his first day he wanted to impress us with the speed of his tyre change. Remember, Kev?"

Kevin smiled and nodded. He was returning to the land of the living.

"There he was with the bolt-removing gun, zapping around as if he was at Brand's Hatch. And then he's pulling at this wheel when Kev says –" He held a palm out Kevin.

"Aren't you going to jack it up?"

They all chuckled.

"Snotridge," said Chris. "What a muppet."

They were silent for a moment. Kurt put down his knife and fork. He had finished his meal. Kevin still had a quarter of his roll left.

"Not a single decent Debbie in here," Chris remarked.

Kevin didn't bother looking around.

Chris leaned towards him. "Isn't that one of yours over there, at the table near the dart board? With the poor man's Steve McQueen."

Kevin swung round. His movement caused her to glance at him. It was Beryl. Her expression was neither cold nor welcoming. And he knew that she had seen him and been waiting to give him just that indifferent look.

"Two times," she gasped. "That's never happened before..."

His very own impassive look probably threw her. Or perhaps she had expected it.

The Police's *Message in a Bottle* sprang to mind.

"You're only as young as the woman you feel. Eh, Kev?"

"She's not as young as she looks, Chris."

"Still, she always puts on her best earrings for you."

Kevin gave him raised eyebrows, knowing it was a mistake.

"Her ankles."

Kevin smiled. The others laughed and Chris returned his smile. The corners of his mouth were razor-sharp.

"I thought she'd dropped off the radar?" said Steve.

Kevin nodded.

Was it three weeks ago now? Yes, it must have been. He'd been blind stinking drunk and he staggered to the building in the pouring rain. He'd been out there in the monsoon without an umbrella. Nobody was out in that storm. The infrequent car passed with fountains curling from its wheels: for the roads had been like rivers, the drainage overflowing. And the pavement had been black and shiny. He'd searched the bells at the main door like a person with a serious eye problem. And when he found her name he pressed hard. Above the pelting rain he heard nothing. He wobbled and then staggered back to look up to where he thought her flat should be. There was no light. But it was eleven. Maybe she was asleep. He went back and pressed on her bell.

Under the arch of the doorway it was relatively dry. Two empty milk bottles stood in a corner. The urge to urinate took him and he unzipped. The idea of her finding the bottle made him sneer. He steadied himself with a hand on the wall, and was pleased with the hollow sound, more rounded and satisfying than a kettle filling.

Here's a message in a bottle. Only the next day when he remembered what he had done, did he realise that it would be the milkman who would get the message.

What an idiot he was, he thought.

Beryl was a victim. He couldn't respect her. The mask he

always wore for her was opaque and made of cast iron. She'd get enough glimpses of him to keep coming back for more. But she was unlucky enough to have met him when he hadn't quite got over Sandra. So she found herself unwittingly churned up in the wake of that relationship.

(Pathetic in) My mind's eye

You make me feel so empty
Pathetic in my mind's eye
You quell my lust
Give me a moist thigh

You make me feel so useless
Pathetic in my mind's eye
You dish out your love
Until it's almost a lie

You make me feel so unwanted
Pathetic in my mind's eye
You evade my attentions
Until I want to die

You make me feel so broken
Pathetic in my mind's eye
And I want your love
Is my continual cry

Kurt was telling them about Hamburg and where he worked.
"There's plenty of work there. And I know what you two are on." He was talking to Chris and Kevin. "So I can tell you that you will earn more."
"Yeah, but it's all sausages and sauerkraut," said Chris.
"Food is not an English strong point."
"You put that away sharpish," said Steve looking at Kurt's

empty plate.

"Are you over here recruiting?" asked Chris.

"No," said Kurt. And then to Steve: "*Hunger ist der beste Koch.*" He waited a moment before translating. "Hunger is the best cook."

This stumped them all.

In the silence Chris lit up a cigarette.

Kevin noticed that he hadn't asked whether he'd finished eating. He had, but he would have liked to have been asked. For a moment he contemplated picking up the remains of his baguette, demonstratively peeling back more of the cling film and taking a bite, but the thought of eating appalled him. Chris's smoke was nauseating. He felt hot and a little sick. The baguette was lead in his stomach. He quickly took a sip of his shandy and he was so pleased with the taste that he gulped more than half away.

"Does Mick still give you those puzzles?" said Kurt.

"Yeah," said Chris. "They're as crap as ever."

But Kurt remembered them fondly and would not be crushed.

"Do you remember twenty legs and flies?" he asked.

After handing out the work chits Mick had asked them what had twenty legs and flies. For the best part of the morning suggestions were shouted out. Among the better suggestions were hybrid caterpillar-butterflies and a flock of ten birds. Everything else was simply bizarre. At the lunchtime break Mick put them out of their misery, only to immediately give them another. As always Mick reminded them of the question, as if they could have forgotten.

"What has twenty legs and flies?" he asked. "Ten pairs of trousers."

The groans were loud, the disappointment louder.

Mick grinned from one to the other. Then he asked: "What has four legs and flies?"

"Two pairs of trousers," rebounded back. Mick just shook his head.

"Mick's an idiot," said Chris.

"He keeps the place happy," said Kurt.

"And he has our respect," added Kevin.

Chris had no answer. He leant back and took a long satisfying drag on his cigarette.

At the garage Chris was the bodywork man. He could make a write-off look like a new car. All of them were car mechanics, but each of them had a specialisation. Chris thought he was too good for the garage. He had ambition. With enough money he wanted to set up his own business.

Kurt was again talking of his workplace. The garage sounded efficient and modern, a real conveyor belt operation. Mick's garage was a dirty chaos. Yet, his philosophy of the customer not being a number kept the work coming in. The garage had a good reputation and it was all Mick's doing.

"Hamburg's just over an hour's flight away," said Kurt. "So popping over for the weekend is not out of the question. You don't need to use up your holiday."

After the holiday Sandra and Kevin went their separate ways. They met only once, weeks after they had broken up.

At the end of the evening he walked her to the station. Parting was difficult. He gave her a peck on the cheek and she stood as if expecting more. Then fat tears rolled down her face.

He had not been cruel, but he had been distant, not giving their intimacy a chance to look in. They'd met on mutual ground. Not no man's land; they were not at war.

She too had put on a brave face.

"Why are you crying?" he asked.

"It's so sad."

They hugged and all he could manage was a kiss on the hair behind her ear. She disengaged herself, straightened her clothing, smiled, but avoided looking at him.

"Goodbye, Kevin."

"Bye, Sandra." His words were out before he could think.

She turned and he watched her disappear down the steps.

He wheeled about and walked away. Thoughts of her tears

stopped him after twenty paces. Then he turned and ran back to the station. He bounded down the steps. But he wasn't sure which way she had gone. He ran through the labyrinth of the underground station, desperate, like a headless chicken. He didn't find her and he left, beaten. Beaten, his shoulders sagging, he felt like a sad beaten dog. He knew how he must have looked, but it was how he felt and how he wanted to be. And a part of him said that it was meant to be like this. It was right that he should not find her.

"And for the treasure-trove we had to collect a comic king of the jungle," said Kurt. Somehow talk had returned to treasure hunts. Chris had gone to the toilet.

"A what?" said Steve.

"Kevin got it," said Kurt. "We had no idea."

"So what was it?"

Kurt looked to Kevin, obviously wanting him to bask in his glory. Kevin couldn't bask, but for Kurt's sake, he obliged.

"A dandy lion."

Steve was quiet for a minute. "I get the king of the jungle bit, but where's the comic b - ah yeah. Jeez. That's good."

Chris returned during further treasure hunt highlights. Kurt, who was obviously enjoying reminiscing, drove the conversation. Until he looked at the clock on the wall and gave Kevin a slight nod.

"We'd better get you to the station then," said Kevin.

"When's your train?" asked Chris.

"Around three."

"Time for another quick one."

"I don't want to be pissed at the airport," said Kurt.

"I thought you were skint," said Kevin.

"I thought the loaded German might buy a round for his buddies."

"I don't want another," said Kevin.

They turned to Steve.

"I'm easy."

Kevin began to grow angry. Chris was pushing it and

Steve sitting on the fence. Their typical characters were being summed up in this single moment.

"He doesn't live here, so he's the guest," said Kevin, "you should buy him one."

"I'll buy you a drink," said Steve magnanimously.

Kevin tightened.

"Thanks Steve," said Kurt, "but I don't want another."

"I'll have one," said Chris.

Kevin pounced before Steve could answer. "He wasn't offering you one."

The two eyed one another. Kevin was not spoiling for a fight, but he wasn't going to give an inch either.

Then Chris smiled. "Keep your hair on, Kev. It's only a drink."

"Yeah, and who's getting their knickers in a twist trying to pump a drink from a friend?"

"I've got to go," said Kurt.

"Yes," said Steve. "I've got things to do."

Kevin was angry with Steve too. But Steve was the kind of guy, like Kurt in many ways, you couldn't be angry with. He was a good guy and no threat. He sought compromise and not confrontation. There was a lot of woman in him.

Kurt got up. Steve followed.

"Jesus Kev," said Chris, picking up his cigarettes and car keys and getting up, "no wonder you're always ending up in a fight."

"Leave it out," said the stranger's girlfriend.

But the stranger didn't leave it out.

"I need to go to the loo," said Kurt.

Steve was standing next to Kurt. "It was nice seeing you again."

Kevin rose. "I need to take a leak too."

"See you around, Steve," said Chris. "Kurt. Keep your pecker up - as many as you can." As they shook hands he said: "I'll get that drink next time, eh?"

Kurt smiled.

Then Chris and Kevin were facing one another.

"See you tomorrow," said Chris.

"Yeah."

"Lighten up, Kev."

Kevin barely managed to stop himself exploding. Chris would eventually find out about Sandra's death and then he'd understand. They all would.

Kevin smiled sickly.

The four of them went outside to the entrance where the toilets were located. Steve and Chris nodded or waved their goodbyes again.

Kurt had shouldered his holdall. In the toilets he stopped and looked around. "I'm not putting this down in here."

Kevin was at the urinals.

"I'll wait for you outside," said Kurt. "I want to do the business." Before leaving he added: "I don't want to wave the wobbly willy at the white-washed walls."

He laughed and Kevin smiled. The words harked back to some joke he no longer remembered.

Kevin scanned the wall for new graffiti. He reread: "I gave Linda Lovelace a sore throat." Underneath that was written: "I gave Mickey Mouse ear ache." He found: "Too many cocks spoil the brothel." And then: "Every fifteen minutes a man gets knocked down on a British road - and he's getting fed up with it." Nothing new.

He zipped up and washed his hands.

Words, thought Kevin.

He slammed the blow-drier with the heel of his hand.

Words. Wasting away slowly in bed his Dad had time to think. But when he was trying to impart some wisdom, his words measured and even, rehearsed in his mind who knows how many times, they still seemed to come out flat. Kevin couldn't help feeling that it was all so little. This was the sum of his father's life. "All we know is this life, Kev." He huffed and smiled. "And some say that's an illusion. It doesn't matter." He drifted for a moment. "One thing that we can be sure of is that death comes to us all. So make the most of your life." At the time Kevin didn't want his Dad's words. Oh, the portent of them was chiselled in his mind. But they were mere words nonetheless. His Dad's wisdom was his Dad's personal wisdom. Something he couldn't impart. And so Kevin didn't want his words. He didn't want his wisdom. He just wanted his Dad.

Outside he stood beside Kurt's bag.

"I could be a while," said Kurt.

"Take your time."

Kurt looked at him strangely, but didn't say anything.

Shortly after leaving him, as if in a stage play, Beryl came out of the pub with the poor man's Steve McQueen. If he hadn't known how she used make-up, he would have thought she was white with shock at the sight of him. Beryl had a face from another era: the 1920s perhaps. A pillbox hat with a little netting would not have gone amiss. She was a small woman, almost delicate, prim and proper, but only in the way she dressed. Her face was powdered white, her small lips uniformly red. Small dashes of blood in the snow. And the look she gave him was cold.

His gaze was neither cold nor aggressive. It was nothing.

He was glad when she walked on as if she didn't know him.

Maybe she thought he had been ignoring her in the pub. But before Chris had said anything he really hadn't seen her. Argh, let her think what she wanted. Who gives a toss?

He looked down at Kurt's bag, tapped it with his toe.

Beryl went for a chastised Elizabeth I look that he never understood. Of course she fell apart in bed. She became just another floozy. Not prim or proper. And certainly not delicate. Wildcat would be a better description. But when she was done up she reminded him of his primary school teacher Mrs. McDonald. Not that he was ever attracted to Mrs. McDonald. On the contrary. They'd called her the Duck. And to most of the pupil's her wide protruding lips and chin made her resemble a duck. What disgusted Kevin was that she always managed to smear lipstick on her teeth. He hated her for it. He didn't like her near him. And she was always hovering near him, because he did badly in her class. Where was she now? At a pinch she could have been born in the twenties. She was no doubt long retired. Maybe she was dead. Or still eating her way through lipsticks?

When he looked up Beryl and McQueen were twenty paces or so away. They weren't holding hands.

Kevin smiled. *Message in a bottle.*

There were more clouds in the sky, but it was still warm.

Two lads, student types with arms that were puny, prospects that were promising, left the pub laughing.

Of course Beryl was a born victim. Or maybe she was just a victim with him. Maybe she played victim to his brutal sadist. And he wouldn't let her get out of her role. McQueen didn't look as if he had the upper hand. Maybe she was the torturer and he her victim. With Sandra the roles had always been in a state of flux. He the killer, she the killed. He trampled upon and left to die, she marching on. And then united, together, tender, soft, loving.

When he looked up he saw Beryl striding towards him. McQueen was waiting way off next to a lamppost. An invisible leash tied him to it. Beryl looked determined, angry. Kevin could hear the Duck about to give him a piece of her mind. "You'll amount to nothing, if you don't pull your socks up, young man."

It was too late to look away, so he dulled himself, letting his eyes become empty, his brow easy.

He had once said to her that she had sad eyes and she replied: "So have you." Pah, you wish, he said to himself.

And when she'd helped him roll up the carpet in his flat he had said: "huh, just like a married couple." He couldn't help looking at her to relish her feeling. He knew saying such a thing did her in. He was a cruel bastard. And now he regretted saying it. He should not be such a bastard. Of course he didn't generally feel sorry for saying it. He only felt sorry at this moment. The moment would pass. It always did.

She hadn't forgotten something in the pub. She was

coming directly towards him. Was she going to ask him about the milk bottle? Had she been in after all?

She stopped in front of him, standing close, as if to stop him escaping. Or to stop him slipping passed with the basketball. But her expression said that she was not playing.

"I've found somebody," she said.

He nodded his head slightly. She waited.

Her little teeth were white, not ivory, really white, with not a smear of lipstick in sight.

"Good," he eventually said.

"You really mean that, don't you?"

"I said it, didn't I?"

She would forever be his victim: caught in the backlash of his relationship with Sandra. Forever chained and whipped. She'd failed the acid test from the start. She'd phoned the day after they'd met, effectively handing him the keys to the chains.

"You really don't care."

He didn't have an answer. His feeling sorry for her was evaporating rapidly. Leaving him solid and stone-like.

"Well, you can sod off, Kevin."

She was breaking free and he was going to let her. The door was open. As far as he was concerned it always had been. Deep down he knew it had not. He had stood in the way: feigning a need for her, doing her in with a date as if they were girlfriend and boyfriend. He'd always stood in the way. And he argued that she had never complained. But in truth he had chosen not to hear her when she had complained.

"Just leave mc alone, okay?"

She wanted drama but he didn't have drama for her.

"Sure." Yes, he would let her go. He'd cheated her out of her love and sex long enough. And then again, he wasn't sure. In the sober light of day it was easy to make such resolutions. But would he leave her alone? Did she really want to be left alone?

A couple left the pub, but Beryl didn't move. She was trying to snare his eyes.

He let her have them, but only furtively. For he realised

that she could misinterpret them. Damn it, the sorrow she could see was not for their relationship.

There was movement behind him and she looked away. He knew Kurt had appeared. Funny, he hadn't heard the rush of the blow drier, but now he heard it.

"Goodbye, Kevin."

He heard the echo of Sandra's voice. And he saw the back of Sandra disappear down the steps. She didn't turn around. Just walked out of his life. And now out of life.

"Bye, Beryl."

She stared at him and the seconds ticked by. Then she turned and walked back to her new jailer. Or maybe it wasn't like that. Maybe she had the upper hand? Maybe they –

"What was that all about?" asked Kurt.

"Don't ask."

Kurt shouldered his bag and Kevin knew he had watched Beryl, however absently, for too long. He'd worn an opaque and iron mask for her. Maybe he had been a prisoner too. No, he could choose to remove the mask. But when he was with her he never had, not really. He had adopted a role he thought he could shed.

"Just something getting kicked into touch," he said, as they began walking in the opposite direction.

"I thought Steve said she'd dropped off the radar."

"Yeah. That's what Steve said."

They walked in silence for a time.

Kevin raked his mind for something to say. The best he could do was: "What time do you have to be a station, again?"

"The train's at three. Be there, a quarter to, I guess."

Silence fell upon them again.

"What was that with Chris?" said Kurt.

"Chris is a wanker. The guy just bugs me sometimes."

"Yeah, I know what you mean."

When Kurt had worked at Mick's Chris had often goaded him. Kurt was easy meat, but that didn't stop Chris from riding him. It often got Kevin's goat. "But I have to work with him."

Silence.

Kevin suddenly realised that Kurt could think he was sad because of what had just happened with Beryl.

"She didn't mean that much to me."

He looked at Kurt, but his profile gave nothing away.

"She wasn't my girlfriend or anything."

"Have you got a girlfriend?"

Kevin wasn't sure how to answer. "No."

"You should come over to Hamburg again. There are some fine women there."

"Yeah." Kevin didn't want to bring Kurt down. He wanted his lightness. "Are you talking dirty weekend?"

"If you like."

"The last time we did that we didn't get any nookie. The only thing dirty about it was that bloody room."

Kurt laughed. "That was a long time ago."

Kevin's own laughter died before it started.

"I don't like Rod Steward," said Kurt. "But most of all that song."

"*Sailing*?" said Kevin and he launched into it in the best rasping voice he could muster. But he couldn't keep it up.

"Stop it," Kurt pleaded.

It had topped the charts at the time and they had danced to it with the girls.

"How long did we spend trying to persuade them to come back with us?" asked Kurt.

"I don't know."

"It was ages."

"Yeah. Freezing our buts off."

Kevin could feel Kurt enjoying the memory. His own recall was fleeting. He simply couldn't get there to relive it. It was such a long time ago, about ten years, and so much had happened since then.

"I don't even remember their names," said Kevin.

Kurt smiled. Maybe he didn't remember their names either. Whatever, Kevin's words put paid to further excavation.

He hadn't wanted to crush Kurt, but he knew he had sounded bitter.

"What's up, Kev?"

"I'm just tired," he said. "Maybe a little fed up." He really hadn't made as good an impersonation of himself as he thought at the pub.

"But it's still fun at the garage?"

"Sure."

"No one has found the money making idea?"

"Not yet." Then something uplifting occurred to Kevin. "We're still working on the Tardis."

Kurt laughed and Kevin was pleased and smiled.

To get through the day they had sometimes come up with madcap ideas for ways of making money. They agreed to grow their hair long and sell it for wigs. One of the lads suggested going house to house with his sister's guinea pigs. They could mow the lawn and get fed too.

Then an apprentice said: "Wouldn't it be really good if we could build a Tardis, like in Doctor Who?"

The lads laughed and he was hurt.

"No, not a time machine," he said hurriedly. "That's silly. But we're all engineers -"

"Car mechanics," someone corrected.

"Yes. But we're not stupid. If we put our heads together we could do it."

"What are you talking about?"

"I'm saying that we build something that is bigger on the inside than it is on the outside."

"Oh, that's okay then."

"Yeah. I really thought you wanted to build a time machine. Silly me."

The laughter was mingled with querulous looks.

"Come on Kev," said Kurt, "you are good at putting things together."

"Yeah. I'll have to work on that one."

They walked over the bridge and waited for a gap in the

traffic to cross the road. This was the ring road from the motorway. It was always busy. Every day was a Monday morning. Even a Sunday.

The clouds above them were light but unbroken: not a patch of blue was to be seen.

"My father's garage is bigger than Mick's. We have fun, but it's not got that family atmosphere."

"I know what you mean," said Kevin. "Mick keeps the show rolling."

"So," said Mick, towards the end of the day. "What has four legs and flies?"

The best suggestion was gliding monkeys. But Mick pointed out that they were not flying.

With no more guesses forthcoming Mick said: "a dead horse."

"It wasn't always fun at Mick's," said Kurt, above the sound of traffic.

Kevin immediately thought of the break-in, but Kurt was elsewhere.

"There was that big bloke, remember?"

"Nobby?"

Kevin had forgotten about him.

Mick had told them on Friday that Nobby was returning on Monday after a two-year absence. He was a distant relative of Mick's wife. He had suffered a mental breakdown, but now felt fit enough to work. Kurt and Kevin had never met him. That Monday the stigma of the mental breakdown made the lads wary. Mick appeared overly jolly. Boisterous and annihilating. The lads went the opposite way. They treated Nobby with padded gloves: overly considerate, too kind. Nobby kept himself to himself, speaking when spoken too, and one could have thought him shy. The gentle giant type. But no one was totally at ease. And then one day, after a few weeks, he didn't come into work. Two days later Mick told them he'd committed suicide. Although they'd done nothing wrong, they all felt somehow guilty.

Suicide. Shit. So many people cling on to life. Would give

everything for a little bit more.

And outside his Dad's bedroom he sniffed and swallowed a gob of snot. It was horrible. And he promised God to swallow a gob of snot every day, every hour. Only if his father could live. The quacks had failed; science articles spoke of promises, the future, but not now. Only God was left. And he believed in him as much as he did in Father Christmas. But He was all Kevin had left. Oh, God take my arm. Take a leg. But please, please, don't take him.

"Poor guy," said Kurt, as they ascended the hill, leaving the sound of the traffic behind them.

Kevin didn't say anything. He wasn't sure what he felt for Nobby. Pity? Anger? He'd hardly known him.

"Kurt, I have to tell you something?" said Kevin before he knew it. He hadn't prepared anything. He certainly hadn't made a conscious decision to tell his friend now, as they went up the hill. He wasn't sure whether he had decided to tell him at all. And why now? Why not when Kurt had thought he was sad about Beryl? Why not in the safety of the flat? In the car on the way to the station? When parting? No, not then. That would be crass.

Kurt waited.

And now Kevin felt he couldn't say it. "Do you remember Sandra?" He almost choked on her name. Kurt was looking at him, but he stared straight ahead, fixing his gaze on the small green window frame of the house at the top of the hill, at the mouth of the alleyway out of the cul-de-sac. A bathroom window? A toilet window?

"Yes."

Kevin wasn't sure he could bring himself to say the words. His jaw seemed as set as his gaze. His mind petrified.

"Yes," said Kurt again.

Kevin sighed as if he had been holding his breath. But going up the hill laboured his breathing.

"I heard today." Come on, come on. "That she'd been run over."

Kurt waited for more, before asking: "Is she okay?"

Kevin couldn't answer. He couldn't say no. Some limit within him had been reached. He felt Kurt looking so he shook his head. And even this gesture took him to the edge.

Kurt was silent and Kevin wondered whether he was remembering the drunken night in the *Kneipe*. After all, that was all Kurt had of Sandra: a name and second hand information. Ah, but what information. Love lost. There again, Kurt had been drunk too. How much did he remember? Probably a lot. Kevin wasn't one for pouring out his heart. Certainly not to a guy. So he believed.

"I'm sorry," said Kurt. They were silent for a few steps. "That's terrible."

Kevin led the way into the alleyway at the top of the cul de sac.

"Can you tell me what happened?"

Shit no.

Kurt held his tongue for the length of the alleyway. When they emerged at the end of another cul de sac he asked: "Do you want to talk about it?"

"No," said Kevin. His bluntness was aggressive and he didn't want to be angry. "Not now," he added.

Kurt plunged back into thought.

They walked in silence.

Up here walking parallel to the road below was peaceful suburbia. The sound of traffic was almost a memory. But for them the street was deserted. It was truly a sleepy Sunday afternoon. And that's what Kevin wanted. He wanted to sleep. He felt dog-tired and he didn't want to face the world. He didn't even feel up to driving his friend to the station. Could he give him the car keys? No. That was absurd.

"Wherever she is now," Kurt began. Kevin was startled. He didn't want his words. He wanted silence. "I'm sure she'd want you to get on with your life."

His words confused Kevin. Wherever she was now? Did she have to be somewhere else? Was it inconceivable that she simply no longer existed?

"This is not how I want to remember you," his Dad had said. Boys don't cry.

I'm sure she'd want you to get on with your life. Did Kurt think he was contemplating topping himself?

"I can't help you," said Kurt.

Kevin acknowledged him with a nod. The concern in his friend's voice was a comfort. He didn't want his friend worrying and he sought something uplifting.

Even the crumpled grey blanket of the sky seemed to have conspired against him. He laughed. "What have you done with the sun?"

Kurt gave him a queer look. Even when his smile came it didn't dispel the confusion in his face.

"It's all a bit of a merry-go-round," Kevin said.

He knew Kurt didn't know where he was coming from, but he didn't elaborate. He wasn't sure why he had said it. Did he mean his state? Or was he making a comment on life in general?

He was losing it.

"Don't worry, Kurt. I'm okay."

"I can see that."

For some reason Kevin found this hilarious. He burst into laughter. And this time his friend's confusion was overwhelmed and he too chuckled.

"No, I'm all right," he said, when he'd recovered. "Really."

His two-storey block was in sight. He had an upper flat.

"Tell me," he began. "Did you mean that in the pub about the money we could earn?"

Kurt perked up. "Of course. I can't say it'll be double, but at least a third more."

"There's the language problem."

"You've been there. Everyone likes to speak English. But you're right. You'd have to learn German."

Kevin dug into his pocket for his keys.

"Of course you have the advantage of being bilingual already," said Kurt.

Kevin stopped at the main door. "How's that?"

"English and bullshit."

Kevin laughed. "Where'd you get that one from?"

"Experience."

"Funny. Real funny." He opened the door.

They climbed the stairs in silence.

Kevin opened the flat door and was caught by the flashing of the answer-phone. He decided to ignore it. Kurt followed him in.

"Time for a coffee?"

"Not really."

"I guess not." He strode across the room, glad that he'd turned his pad of drunken writing over. "I'll just get my car keys, then." He looked over his shoulder before going into the bedroom. The flat door was ajar. Kurt had dumped his bag in the middle of the room. He was looking around.

It wasn't a dump. It was orderly. Maybe dusty in places, but hey, this was a bachelor's pad.

Kevin plucked his car keys from the bowl on top of the chest of drawers. In the bowl were his rings and the gold bracelet Sandra had given him one Christmas. His name was engraved on it.

"I'll leave you my card," said Kurt. He was at the dining table when Kevin came out.

"Very posh."

Kurt picked up the pen and began writing on the back. "Here's my private number." Kevin tossed his car keys in the air and caught them with the same hand.

"I think I've got it somewhere."

"I've moved."

He handed it to Kevin and for the first time since leaving the pub there was eye contact.

"In case you want to talk."

"Great." And they both knew that there would be no contact until Kurt came by again.

Kevin put it in his back pocket.

"Let's go," he said.

Kurt picked up his bag and they moved towards the door. "You got yourself a nest here, I think you're waiting for a woman to come along and feather it."

"And clean it," said Kevin.

"Kevin," said Sandra, "you slob."

They laughed. Then Kurt noticed the blinking light of the answer phone. "Aren't you going to listen to your call?"

"No." But then it could be important. Sandra's sister? Or her husband? His Mum? Unlikely, unless she'd spoken in a hurtling tizz. Or someone else who had heard? And Kurt knew, after all. "Have we time?"

"Easy."

Kevin pushed the flat door to an inch of being closed before pressing the play messages button.

After the introductory date and time Rita came on the line. "Kevin. Are you there? Pick up." In the pause that followed, her breathing was full of frustration and some surprise. "Where are you? Oh God." She sounded urgent. "Call me when you're back. It's urgent." She hung up.

"You want to call her?"

"No," said Kevin. He did wonder what could be so urgent. She sounded fine. Albeit, frustrated that he was not in. But she was not distressed. Maybe something had happened to her son. That would be too much for Kevin. One lot of devastating news was enough for the day, the month, the year.

Whereas Beryl was a girl, Rita was a real woman. She was voluptuous and full of passion. But she came as a package. She had a small fair-haired boy called Justin. A sweet kid of about two. Everyone carried baggage. Hers was evident. Kevin was carrying a load too. And now he carried the further burden of Sandra's death.

They left the flat and Kevin led Kurt to his GTI.

"Still two-timing the women, then?"

"I'd be two-timing if one was a girlfriend."

At times juggling the two women had been hectic, but never stressful. Justin was Rita's ball and chain. That meant she relied on Kevin visiting. And when he did take Rita out he avoided the pubs and clubs Beryl frequented. He took Rita to the Christmas do. Mick and the lads were overwhelmed.

"New wheels, eh?" said Kurt.

"About a year ago," he said, unlocking the car. "Chuck your bag on the back seat."

The radio boomed into life the minute he turned the ignition. He'd fitted an extra set of state-of-the-art speakers in the back. Kevin quickly turned it off.

Kurt spoke again as they drove down the hill.

"Sunroof too."

"Don't touch it," said Kevin. "You have a liking for wearing unusual things." To sound unnatural and affected Kevin had contemplated saying inclined to, prone to or partial to. Like in the pub when Chris had used the word altercation and Steve had used the word sanguine, Kevin had been on the verge of saying: how very droll. But he hadn't been in the humour and the moment had passed. For some toff such language would be okay, but he and the lads didn't need such pretences, unless in jest. "Like wearing frog suits," Kevin said.

"Never to be forgotten," said Kurt. "I still think -"

"I know. But no."

"Bird-shit."

"Yes," laughed Kurt, "and after all that bloody polishing too."

"Marmalade."

Kurt smiled. "What happened to your Bantam?"

Kurt had tried to keep up with the lads in the early days. At a midweek after-work session he had overdone it and was in no state to get home. He needed help and no one was offering. In the end Kevin took him back to his bed-sit. There he dumped him on the sofa, taking only his shoes off, covering him with a blanket and the surrounding floor with newspaper. He even put his kitchen sink bowl on the floor next to his head.

The next morning they were both up late. There wasn't even time to shower before work. Kurt was parched and hungry.

They bolted their coffees after adding cold water. Kevin wolfed down his toast, but Kurt could only nibble his one.

"Leave it," said Kevin.

"I have to eat something," Kurt said.

"Bring it with you."

At the time Kevin had a motorbike: a BSA Bantam 175. They set off. Kurt tried to eat his toast, but it was impossible. So he held it away from himself as they sped along the street. When they arrived at the garage the toast had been stripped of marmalade. Some of it was smeared on Kurt's collar.

"It's at my mother's. I keep it ticking over."

"I think you spent more time tinkering with that bike than you did with your birds."

"I don't know which was more reliable. I held that bike together with string and elastic bands. Those relationships with less."

They fell silent.

"I'm happy in Hamburg," said Kurt suddenly. "I have friends, but a pal like you would be great. I mean, somebody you can talk to."

"I know what you mean," said Kevin.

"It's only when I'm here that I feel like that. It's like belonging."

"Sounds like homesickness."

"No. I'm happy. It's like I want you and Mick and the garage, all of you, in Hamburg."

"We went through a lot together."

They all saw him clamber down the stairs from the office. None of them looked at him directly. They also knew Mick had sacked him. They suspected he had form and nobody understood why Mick had taken him on. They'd christened him Captain Pugwash. Not to his face, of course. He was a tattooed bullet-head with a bulldog face and a pit-bull demeanour. More brawn than brains. The lug was hard-wired from the neck up. He'd not fitted in and lasted only a week. If Pugwash had done porridge, Mick wouldn't say. Since the time he'd told them of Nobby's breakdown, he'd never divulged the past of new employees.

Although nobody looked at him directly, they all saw him fetch the large monkey wrench. By the time he was heading for the stairs, they had exchanged looks and were converging on him, tools in hand. Rather than make a dash for the stairs Pugwash chose to stand his ground. One against five.

"Who's first for some brain surgery, then?" he said.

Everyone remained still. The ape was surrounded, but with the monkey wrench lightly chopping the air, he was still dangerous.

Mick appeared at the top of the stairs.

"Let him get his stuff lads. The police are on their way."

After a moment the lug straightened and dropped the spanner. The silence had been enough to hear a pin drop so the wrench clanging on the concrete floor was shattering.

They opened a way to the locker room.

"This is not the end of it," he growled to Mick.

If there were any repercussions Kevin never heard of them.

There was no parking at the station. Kevin pulled up just beyond the entrance at the loading area. He dropped into neutral but left the engine running.

"I could park back at the bus station and we could walk. I want to get a video, anyway."

"No. There's no time," said Kurt. He had ten minutes and the walk would cut it fine.

Kurt turned awkwardly in his seat to extend his hand.

"It was good seeing you again, Kev."

"You too."

"Thanks for the lift."

"No sweat."

There was a pause and then Kurt looked at him so sincerely that Kevin felt uncomfortable. "Take care of yourself."

"You too."

"And if you're ever passing through Hamburg look me up."

"It's a deal."

Kurt climbed out and grabbed his bag. He turned at the station entrance and waved a single wave. Kevin nodded and then Kurt was gone.

Kevin pushed the car into gear and pulled out into the traffic on the road.

The sense of loss was surprising. One minute they were together and then he was gone. Didn't they have so much more to say?

He circled back to the bus station and found a parking place in front of the video hire shop.

Kurt was a good lad, he thought. No, he was more than that; he was a good friend. They hadn't seen each other for more than a year, but it clicked as if they'd seen each other only yesterday. Kevin realised that he didn't have such a close friend. Steve perhaps. But Kurt was on his wavelength. That's why they could spend a weekend together chasing women. Steve was too straight for such gallivanting. He was the serious type. A woman would come along, they'd get married and have their two-point-one kids, and that would be that. Kevin knew Steve enjoyed the stories of his female conquests. But the envy he showed was not genuine. For Steve could never be like him.

There were three or four pigeons squabbling over a piece of something. One had only one foot. Kevin had a theory that every group of pigeons had a one-footed veteran.

Picture of Progress

Smooth tall panels
So white, so hygienic
Vast constructed sections
Technology in its glory

Not a door in sight
Marvellous building
Smoked glass crest

Awe-struck admirers

Gardens green all around
All at peace not a sound
Not even the weeping
Of the headless sparrow

In the hire shop he nodded to the kid behind the counter. Were they getting younger or was he getting older?

He checked the bin of used "for sale" videos. Nothing grabbed him. Then he wandered the shelves. He needed something to get him through the evening. Normally he went for action or harrowing films. But he wasn't up to it. He needed something to absorb him, something to take him away from himself. And he wasn't into light films: frivolous comedies, love stories, costume dramas and the like. But he would need something uplifting. Difficult, if you ruled out comedies.

In the horror section he found "An American Werewolf in London." He decided to risk it.

"It's quite good," said the lad at the counter, as he handed back Kevin his membership card and passed him the video.

"That's not what happened," said Sandra.

"It is," he insisted.

"You've got the wrong film," she said.

Kevin let her have the last word before shoving the video into the player and sitting himself next to her on the sofa.

They watched the entire film. When the end credits began Sandra said again: "See."

"Okay, you were right," he said, pressing stop and then fast-forward on the remote control. "You're like a bloody elephant."

"What?" she said angrily.

He laughed. "I didn't mean you look like an elephant."

She tensed and folded her arms.

"I meant you remember everything."

She relaxed.

"And you've got a great mammary too."

She shrieked with laughter. He smiled and then they kissed.

"Which one?" she asked, when they stopped kissing.

"What do you mean?" he asked.

"My breasts."

He looked down, careful not to bang her head. They were still embraced.

"I can't remember. My memory is terrible. Remember?"

"That's true."

"I'll have to have another look."

"Come on, then."

His hard-on began as she took off her tank top. When she unhooked her bra he was in physical pain.

"I'll have to have a closer look," he said, slipping off the sofa onto the floor.

Within two minutes they were making love, first on the sofa, then on cushions on the floor.

Kevin threw the videocassette on the passenger seat and pulled out of his parking place. The pigeons were gone.

The clouds had gathered into a dark brooding mass and he switched on his lights.

As he drove back to the flat he wondered about Rita's call.

"Where are you?" she said after the pause. She didn't try to hide her annoyance. "Oh God. Call me when you're back. It's urgent."

What was so urgent? She didn't sound as if something terrible had happened. She sounded as if the terrible thing was simply that he was not in.

Would he phone her? No. He wanted to sleep. He had planned the rest of the day. First he'd have a kip and then he'd do some mundane chore, maybe ironing - cleaning? No - and after eating he'd settle down to watch the video with a whisky or three. No, Rita didn't fit in with his plan.

All this was, of course, crap. He knew he was afraid to call her. He was afraid he would open up. It would be just what she wanted. She'd just love to dig her talons deeper into him.

The heavens opened and the downpour was as if someone was on the car roof tipping buckets of water down the front windscreen. He set the wipers to their highest frequency and slowed down. The drains couldn't take the water away fast enough and the road was like a stream.

The rain didn't abate, even when he was parked. He sat in the car for a few moments, before deciding to make a dash for it.

He couldn't open the main door quick enough. But he was already soaked to the skin. His T-shirt clung to him and the cassette case was outlined under it.

In his flat he switched on the lights, took off his shoes and put them on the mat by the door. He padded across the room to the bathroom, placing the videocassette on the dining table as he went passed. Removing his T-shirt was like trying to remove a layer of skin. He was afraid he'd rip it. Eventually he had the sodden thing off. He threw it in the bath. The dolphins were crumpled. Then, sitting on the edge of the bath he vigorously rubbed his hair with a towel.

The same thing had happened yesterday. He'd got drenched after leaving Helen.

He returned the towel to the rail on the wall without getting up. And, although he felt a chill, he sat there looking at it.

What gets wet as it dries? A towel. Mick didn't always win. No, he didn't. What gets bigger the more you take away from it? They got that one eventually. Chris or Martin said: "a hole." And what carries water but is full of holes. Kevin, sussed that one. A sponge.

In the pub, he had been distant, but he had felt alive at the pub. Yes, everything went on as if nothing had changed. And for all them in the pub nothing had changed. And he had felt at ease with Kurt. Now he was alone in his flat: just him and his thoughts. He didn't just feel cold. He felt weary and depressed.

He knew he wasn't going to be good alone.

"Fuck it," he said aloud.

Could he watch the video now? Then what would he do

later? His watch showed three-thirty.

He'd follow his plan. He'd have a lie down.

Kevin left the bathroom and went to the bedroom, where he pulled on another T-shirt. At the window he saw a break in the sky. The rain had turned to a drizzle.

"Typical," he said. His jeans were wet too, but he didn't change them. He looked at the bed. His quilt cover was thrown back, the bed sheet crumpled, everything just as he had left it. Petrified.

"Yeah?"

"Hallo, Kevin."

"Hi Mum. What's up?"

"Kevin, I've got some bad news."

He needed something to warm himself up. He'd make a drink and then lie down.

He waited for a moment and then he returned to the lounge. But he didn't go to the kitchen. Instead he found himself at the answer phone where he played Rita's message again. If it was so urgent, she would have phoned again. There were no new messages.

He dialled Rita's number. When he heard it ringing he began hoping that she wouldn't be in. She picked up after two rings.

"Hallo?" She was out of breath.

"It's me."

"Oh, hallo Kevin." She was pleased.

"You called," he said flatly.

"Yes," the bounce in her voice disappearing. "What are you doing?"

"I was watching a towel dry."

Pause. Oh, why had he phoned? There was no urgency. There was certainly no bad news.

"Well, that sounds interesting." And she chuckled, trying to get him to see the absurdity of watching a towel dry. But Kevin gave her silence. "Are you okay?"

"Yeah."

wanted. She'd just love to dig her talons deeper into him.

The heavens opened and the downpour was as if someone was on the car roof tipping buckets of water down the front windscreen. He set the wipers to their highest frequency and slowed down. The drains couldn't take the water away fast enough and the road was like a stream.

The rain didn't abate, even when he was parked. He sat in the car for a few moments, before deciding to make a dash for it.

He couldn't open the main door quick enough. But he was already soaked to the skin. His T-shirt clung to him and the cassette case was outlined under it.

In his flat he switched on the lights, took off his shoes and put them on the mat by the door. He padded across the room to the bathroom, placing the videocassette on the dining table as he went passed. Removing his T-shirt was like trying to remove a layer of skin. He was afraid he'd rip it. Eventually he had the sodden thing off. He threw it in the bath. The dolphins were crumpled. Then, sitting on the edge of the bath he vigorously rubbed his hair with a towel.

The same thing had happened yesterday. He'd got drenched after leaving Helen.

He returned the towel to the rail on the wall without getting up. And, although he felt a chill, he sat there looking at it.

What gets wet as it dries? A towel. Mick didn't always win. No, he didn't. What gets bigger the more you take away from it? They got that one eventually. Chris or Martin said: "a hole." And what carries water but is full of holes. Kevin, sussed that one. A sponge.

In the pub, he had been distant, but he had felt alive at the pub. Yes, everything went on as if nothing had changed. And for all them in the pub nothing had changed. And he had felt at ease with Kurt. Now he was alone in his flat: just him and his thoughts. He didn't just feel cold. He felt weary and depressed.

He knew he wasn't going to be good alone.

"Fuck it," he said aloud.

Could he watch the video now? Then what would he do

later? His watch showed three-thirty.

He'd follow his plan. He'd have a lie down.

Kevin left the bathroom and went to the bedroom, where he pulled on another T-shirt. At the window he saw a break in the sky. The rain had turned to a drizzle.

"Typical," he said. His jeans were wet too, but he didn't change them. He looked at the bed. His quilt cover was thrown back, the bed sheet crumpled, everything just as he had left it. Petrified.

"Yeah?"

"Hallo, Kevin."

"Hi Mum. What's up?"

"Kevin, I've got some bad news."

He needed something to warm himself up. He'd make a drink and then lie down.

He waited for a moment and then he returned to the lounge. But he didn't go to the kitchen. Instead he found himself at the answer phone where he played Rita's message again. If it was so urgent, she would have phoned again. There were no new messages.

He dialled Rita's number. When he heard it ringing he began hoping that she wouldn't be in. She picked up after two rings.

"Hallo?" She was out of breath.

"It's me."

"Oh, hallo Kevin." She was pleased.

"You called," he said flatly.

"Yes," the bounce in her voice disappearing. "What are you doing?"

"I was watching a towel dry."

Pause. Oh, why had he phoned? There was no urgency. There was certainly no bad news.

"Well, that sounds interesting." And she chuckled, trying to get him to see the absurdity of watching a towel dry. But Kevin gave her silence. "Are you okay?"

"Yeah."

"Well, you don't sound it." Concern had replaced her joy.

Silence.

"My ex came by. I wasn't expecting him. He took Justin to the circus." She waited for him to say something. "They won't be back until eight." Silence. "Kevin, I'm free. We could do something together."

"I -" he began, "er, want to be alone." But he didn't want to be alone.

"Why?"

"I just do." He could feel himself faltering.

"You could come here. I've got some new underwear."

Shit.

"I, er, got some bad news, this morning."

There was a pause, then she said: "I'm sorry. Do you want to talk about it?"

"Not really."

"Is it something terrible?" She was a persistent bitch, he thought.

"You remember me telling you about Sandra?"

"Er, yes." Now it was his turn to falter. But she filled the pause. "Something has happened to her, hasn't it?"

"Mmm."

"Something terrible?"

"Yeah," his voice almost a whisper.

Silence.

"Kevin," she began, speaking convincingly, like a mother to a child. "You shouldn't be on your own." He said nothing. "I'm coming round." He froze. "You need company." Still he said nothing. "Okay?"

"Okay," he said, in a very small voice.

"I'll get the four o'clock bus." Now she sounded urgent. She had to get to him before something happened. As if he was suicidal. "I'll be there in about forty minutes."

"Okay."

"See you soon."

"Yeah."

Only when he hung up did he realise that she may have wanted him to drive round to her. She didn't have a car. No money. But she new the bus timetables by heart.

He stood at the phone for a moment and then went to the kitchen. There he checked the kettle again, and switched it on.

"Shit it," he said as dropped a tea bag into a mug he'd fetched. First Kurt and the pub and now this. Talk about out of the frying pan and into the fire. Should he phone her back? Forty minutes.

He went to the sink and looked out of the window. The sky was still full of clouds, but they were light. The storm had passed.

He realised that he had been quite happy with Kurt. Their short time alone was good. It wasn't that Kurt had actively helped him. It was merely his being there for him. Perhaps Kevin had spent too long being morose in the pub. He had been ready to lighten up. And he had told Kurt. Yes, Kurt had been there for him. So, perhaps Rita would help him too. Then again, he felt that there was only so much misery a person could take, after that they cracked. They came out of it. Maybe that was why he had laughed so loud after he had said he was okay and Kurt had said: "I can see that."

Nevertheless Rita wasn't Kurt. She wasn't Beryl either. Rita was headstrong. She was a lot to handle. Huh, hadn't she just forced herself on him? That was why he tried to keep her at arm's length. He could have his way with Beryl, because Beryl was predictable. He knew how she ticked. "Just like a married couple." But Rita was wise to a lot of his tricks. She was older and had been there, seen it, done it. So she could outmanoeuvre him. Kevin enjoyed the challenge. And yes, he often got the better of her. "Kevin, only you. Only you." Why? Because she fell to her knees before him. So that he could become a Giant, like in that poster with James Dean and Elizabeth Taylor. And he couldn't help feeling that in doing so she was looking for a new father for her son.

Somebody outside, a youth, shouted: "Get iiiin."

He wasn't sure where the shout came from. It certainly wasn't from his street. Further down the hill. Maybe from the small playground. In any case Kevin was displaced, because the tone of the words sounded like his name.

His father was in front of him at the water-chute. The lamp turned from red to green and his father was away. He shot round the bend and was gone. Then, probably when he was in the pitch-black part of the tunnel he heard him shout a long: "Keeeeeviiiiiin." Of course, it was meant to be fun, but for an instant Kevin experienced an appalling feeling of separation. His father's slow decay, a terrible living decomposition, offered no such sensation, no such drama. Merely a slow inexorable deterioration: from heavyweight to middleweight, from middleweight to featherweight, and from featherweight to flyweight.

Later he had stood at the top of the same water-chute with Brenda and Tony behind him. Sandra was in front of him standing at the waste-high bar, ready to swing under it. Kevin gave the two behind him a sly smile: a "watch this" look. The back of Sandra's bikini top was tied in a bow, like a shoelace. As the light changed from red to green and as she swung to launch herself into the flow of water down the tube he grabbed a loose end of the bow. Before she reached the bend and disappeared out of sight they saw her fumbling with the skimpy bikini top fluttering in her face, her other arm trying to balance and cover her breasts. "Keeeeeviiiin, yoooouu baaaastaaaard." After that Brenda had insisted on going last. Naturally Sandra gave Kevin an carful. But she couldn't keep the smile off her face when she was doing it.

The kettle clicked off.

He poured the water into the mug and played puppeteer with the tea bag. After he few moments he took the mug to the bin, where he picked out the dripping tea bag and dropped it in.

The inside of the bin didn't look inviting. In any case it was too small.

As far as he could remember, his mother had only been

upset with him twice. Both times were when he was a tearaway.

One time was when he was outside playing hide-and-seek. He'd climbed into the perfect hiding place. The kids of the street searched and searched, his brothers too, passing him many times. But they couldn't find him. Only the call to dinner had made him give up his place. He climbed out of their dustbin. His mother was furious. It wasn't bath day.

And before they moved and had their very own bathroom, bath day was always a palaver. The huge tin bath was positioned in the middle of the room and kettles and pots and pans were poured into it. Then one after the other, youngest first, they were cleaned in the same water.

Kevin went to the bedroom and placed the mug on the bedside cabinet.

He lay on the bed and closed his eyes. He didn't draw the curtains.

"Relax," he said to himself. He was tired, but his mind wouldn't stop.

His thoughts wandered to Rita. There was desperation in her. Maybe she was worried that she wouldn't find anybody for herself and Justin. Maybe she was worried about her age and her looks. She had no cause to worry about the latter. She had fine features and she would age well. Why, she'd be attractive in her fifties.

"Relax."

He glanced at the clock. He'd been lying there for two minutes.

He had promised himself to finish with her the next time they met. There was no future for them. The sex was great; the rest was crap. The vibes had been there from the start. And if he was truthful he would have to admit that she had chatted him up at the party.

Tony and he had crashed the party. The two of them had remained in the pub after the others had left. They found themselves in some kind of drunken friendship, each confessing their tolerance and respect of the other, and relished the newfound bond, neither wanting to be the destroyer. To prolong the evening Tony had suggested going to the party. He knew somebody who had been invited. So they bought a bottle of plonk, which they agreed was cheaper than going to some club, and found the flat.

The press of people allowed them to simply slip in. But it also rendered conversation a shouting match. The lounge was standing or dancing room only. One room, probably a bedroom, where all the furniture appeared to have been shoved, was dim and quiet. There were people sitting on the floor, and on and in-between the furniture. The air was heavy with dope.

"Room for another two?" said Tony.

"Not me mate," said Kevin.

"Come on."

"No. You go ahead. It's not my thing."

Tony was game for everything. Since losing Brenda he seemed to be looking for himself. Hoping alcohol or dope or whatever would open an avenue into himself.

Kevin didn't smoke. He had tried a reefer, but he didn't know it and so he didn't trust it. Also he wanted to remain fit, not taking in poison.

So Kevin found himself alone in a crowd. He fetched a beer in the kitchen and wandered about, standing at the wall, moving along the corridor with direction but not purpose. Everyone appeared to know someone and he contemplated leaving.

He was again in the kitchen, this time eyeing the big pan of chilli con carne, when she spoke.

"Try it," she said. "It's good."

He turned to see a fine looking woman with long dark hair pinned up on her head and amazing blue eyes. She was cutting a sliver of cheese. Her cheekbones were geometrically perfect, lips full and sensuous. Kevin was almost dumbstruck.

A lad came into the kitchen, cracked open a beer and left them alone.

"I can see that," he said. "A ladle that stands in the middle like that says it's serious."

She smiled. "Here," she said handing him a paper plate.

"Will this hold it?"

"Two ladles, max."

"I'm not Max," he said. "Name's Kevin."

She smiled. He took the plate and she held out her hand.

"Rita," she said, as he shook her hand. The brutal overhead strip light brought out the reddish tinge to her dark hair. Funny, in the uncompromising light of day she was definitely a redhead.

Kevin put two ladles of chilli on his plate and she handed him a plastic fork.

A laughing couple entered the kitchen. "All right, Rita?" asked the man.

"Fine, Bill."

Kevin forked a mouthful of chilli and chewed as the couple chose from the spread.

"You're right," he said. "It's a corker."

Rita smiled and he knew he'd reached the balancing point. She hadn't made a move to leave and seemed content to nibble her cheese and piece of French bread.

Bill and the girl left and Kevin and Rita were again alone for a moment.

"So you know a few people here, then?" he said.

"Yes. Most of them."

"I don't know anybody. Well, I came with a mate, but he wants to smoke."

"What's his name?"

"Tony."

"I don't think I know him."

"He knows somebody who was invited."

"Aha. What do you think of it?"

"The chilli?"

"No, the party."

"I was thinking of leaving."

She laughed.

newfound bond, neither wanting to be the destroyer. To prolong the evening Tony had suggested going to the party. He knew somebody who had been invited. So they bought a bottle of plonk, which they agreed was cheaper than going to some club, and found the flat.

The press of people allowed them to simply slip in. But it also rendered conversation a shouting match. The lounge was standing or dancing room only. One room, probably a bedroom, where all the furniture appeared to have been shoved, was dim and quiet. There were people sitting on the floor, and on and in-between the furniture. The air was heavy with dope.

"Room for another two?" said Tony.

"Not me mate," said Kevin.

"Come on."

"No. You go ahead. It's not my thing."

Tony was game for everything. Since losing Brenda he seemed to be looking for himself. Hoping alcohol or dope or whatever would open an avenue into himself.

Kevin didn't smoke. He had tried a reefer, but he didn't know it and so he didn't trust it. Also he wanted to remain fit, not taking in poison.

So Kevin found himself alone in a crowd. He fetched a beer in the kitchen and wandered about, standing at the wall, moving along the corridor with direction but not purpose. Everyone appeared to know someone and he contemplated leaving.

He was again in the kitchen, this time eyeing the big pan of chilli con carne, when she spoke.

"Try it," she said. "It's good."

He turned to see a fine looking woman with long dark hair pinned up on her head and amazing blue eyes. She was cutting a sliver of cheese. Her cheekbones were geometrically perfect, lips full and sensuous. Kevin was almost dumbstruck.

A lad came into the kitchen, cracked open a beer and left them alone.

"I can see that," he said. "A ladle that stands in the middle like that says it's serious."

She smiled. "Here," she said handing him a paper plate.

"Will this hold it?"

"Two ladles, max."

"I'm not Max," he said. "Name's Kevin."

She smiled. He took the plate and she held out her hand.

"Rita," she said, as he shook her hand. The brutal overhead strip light brought out the reddish tinge to her dark hair. Funny, in the uncompromising light of day she was definitely a redhead.

Kevin put two ladles of chilli on his plate and she handed him a plastic fork.

A laughing couple entered the kitchen. "All right, Rita?" asked the man.

"Fine, Bill."

Kevin forked a mouthful of chilli and chewed as the couple chose from the spread.

"You're right," he said. "It's a corker."

Rita smiled and he knew he'd reached the balancing point. She hadn't made a move to leave and seemed content to nibble her cheese and piece of French bread.

Bill and the girl left and Kevin and Rita were again alone for a moment.

"So you know a few people here, then?" he said.

"Yes. Most of them."

"I don't know anybody. Well, I came with a mate, but he wants to smoke."

"What's his name?"

"Tony."

"I don't think I know him."

"He knows somebody who was invited."

"Aha. What do you think of it?"

"The chilli?"

"No, the party."

"I was thinking of leaving."

She laughed.

"But the chilli and you are worth staying for."
"In that order?"
"At the moment, yes."
They laughed.
"What do you do, Kevin?"
"I'm a car mechanic." He scooped up another mouthful. "You?"
"Domestic engineer."
He nodded and tried to look for a ring. She wasn't wearing one.
"I'm divorced," she said.
Obviously she'd seen him looking.
She took up the ensuing silence. "So, what's a good looking man like you doing without a woman? You don't look gay."
"I'm not." He wondered what to say. "I guess I'm full of shit," he said.
She froze, a piece of bread and cheese poised before her open mouth. Her shock was complete.
"Somebody said to me that men at my age are like toilets - "
"Occupied or full of shit," she said.
"Right." He knew it was his turn to fill the growing silence, but the beer made him slower than usual. He finished the chilli, desperately searching for something to say.
"Are you going to have some more?
"I've had enough. Compliments to the chef."
He chucked the fork and plate in the big bin liner at the wall near the window.
"Thanks," she said.
"Did you cook it?"
"Yes."
"Wow. You're not only good-looking, you're talented too."
He picked up his beer.
"Are you going to ask me to dance, then?"

He wasn't up to dancing and he didn't like the music or the press of people. "Yeah. Let's go and dance."

Later, in the room for dancing, when people left and said goodbye to Rita, the penny dropped.

"It's your party," he said.

"Yes." She smiled deliciously. "I told you I know most of them. I invited them. I just didn't know you and your friend Tony." He made to interrupt. "I'm glad you're here."

They kissed. Long and deep.

Somebody shouted: "Go for it, Rita."

In the end she had to kick some of the dope-smokers out. They were her friends and although they grumbled, each took it on the chin.

Kevin discovered later that Tony had seen him sharing a piece of chewing gum with Rita and decided not to interrupt.

That night he worked for his chilli. The sex was rampant. The first time was heated and over rather fast. The second time was better. In the morning he was exhausted, but she was so horny they had a third and fierce session. "That was great," she gasped.

The clock showed that he'd been lying on the bed for ten full minutes. He thought about getting up, but his body was too relaxed. He didn't want to move. Perhaps he couldn't move. He closed his eyes again. And perhaps he told himself to relax. In any case he fell asleep.

"Drive passed them, Kurt," said Martin. "Don't look at them. Kev and me'll take a gander at them."

As they drove by, Martin said to Kevin: "I think we can take them."

Kevin nodded.

One was taller than the other and he looked the business. Kevin thought he looked familiar. His dumpy companion looked a pushover. Each held the handle of a heavily laden sports bag.

"Pull over in front of that van," said Martin. "We'll jump out. You turn around and stop somewhere in the road. And come up from behind them."

Kevin and Martin climbed out under cover of the van. "We'll wait for you to stop," said Martin closing the door.

"You carrying anything?" asked Martin, slipping on a knuckle-duster, as they waited at the van. He had already asked Kurt whether he had anything in the car they could use. Kurt had said that he had some jump cables.

"I could swing them about a bit," said Kurt, when Martin dismissed them.

"Who do you think you are? Bruce Lee? You'll probably hurt yourself - or us. Forget it."

They saw Kurt's car stop further down the road and his warning lights begin to flash.

"Let's go," said Martin. "Act uninterested."

They moved round the front of the van onto the pavement.

Kevin was surprised how close they were to the two men. He really had no time to adjust and look disinterested. Even the two blacks had no time to confer. Dumpy looked scared his eyes white and wide in the dark. The taller one looked hard. He wore that perfected scowl well. Kevin was glad he faced Dumpy.

"Name the seven dwarfs," said Mick. And they got Happy, Sleepy, Dopey, Sneezy and Grumpy. But then came Whiny, Fatty, Nosy and Bossy. They didn't get Bashful and Doc.

Martin hid his knuckle-duster fist at the small of his back. Quite far behind the two men Kurt appeared.

Martin stopped and Kevin did too.

"What have you got in the bag, boys?" said Martin.

The two blacks had also stopped, Dumpy looking at them and then at the familiar-looking taller one.

"What's it to you?" said the taller one.

"Maybe it's clobber from Mick's garage."

"Don't know what you're talking about."

"Then you won't mind us taking a look." Martin dropped his fist so that they could see his knuckle-duster.

Dumpy looked behind. Kurt had stopped a good ten paces from them. He held the biting ends of a jump-cable in each hand.

What a burk, thought Kevin. But the situation was too serious for a smile.

He noticed that the leather at the rivets where the handles met the bag was tearing under the strain. They were a pair of bozos. Fancy carrying heavy tools in a sports bag. Why hadn't they brought a car?

"You think you can take me?" said the taller one, letting go of his handle so that Dumpy tipped and was forced to let go too. The sound of metal on metal and metal on concrete confirmed their suspicions.

"As you like it," said Martin raising his fists.

Kevin readied himself. Then he recognised the taller one. He had come in two weeks ago for a service on his souped-up Ford Capri with the Starsky and Hutch go-faster stripes.

"Kurt, we can take care of this," said Martin. "Right Kev?"

"No sweat."

Then again to Kurt: "Drive back to the garage and get that copper up here. Oh, and tell him to order an ambulance. These two have just announced that they like hospital food."

Dumpy wasn't at all happy. He looked to the taller one and tried to say something. But the taller one was rigid and didn't want his companions whinging.

Kurt hesitated; then turned and hastily returned to his car.

"Come on," Martin said quietly to Kevin. And they moved forward determinedly.

Dumpy broke away like a frightened animal. For such an unhealthy looking lump he moved surprisingly quickly. He dashed between the cars, stumbled into the road, reached the other side and kept on going down the hill.

The tall one looked at them, then the bag. Perhaps there was something in there he could use as a weapon. But he was too late.

He took a step back as they neared and then he too turned and ran.

"Leave him," said Martin, before Kevin could think of

giving chase. "I recognised him."

"Me too. He was at the garage a couple of weeks back."

"Ford crappy, right? We've at least got his license plate." They were at the bag, Martin unzipping it. "The cops can pick him up." The missing items were all there.

"Don't touch them," said Kevin. "Fingerprints."

"Maybe," said Martin. "But I don't think the Bill'll waste their powder."

He woke with a start and looked at the clock. He'd been asleep for about twenty minutes. And he wanted more. But she would be there in about ten minutes and he wanted to be awake. So he pushed himself up to the headrest and drowsily picked up his mug of tea. He sipped it. It was only warm, so he took a good gulp.

His mind was immediately besieged.

"It's Sandra," said his Mum. "Kevin, she's been involved in an accident."

A silhouette moved uncertainly across the road at the lights near HMV. A car bounced off the kerb and hit the dark figure. Chips leapt from the newspaper straight up into the air.

"She didn't suffer," said Tim. "It was instant."

Now he really didn't want to see Rita. He just wanted to sleep. Sleep offered him sanctuary.

He finished his tea and swung his legs off the bed so that he sat. He noticed a cloud of dust peeking out from under the chest of drawers. He swept a foot from side to side and the delicate construction lifted and wafted out of sight.

"You got yourself a nest," said Kurt. "I think you're waiting for a woman to come along and feather it."

"And clean it," said Kevin.

His sardonic smile didn't last.

"Kevin," said Sandra, "you slob. I wanted to hoover here, but -"

"Vacuum clean."

"You know what I mean. But there was a cobweb on your hoo- vacuum cleaner."

He had laughed.

Kevin got up and took his mug to the kitchen sink. Then he went into the lounge. The silence was not as oppressive as before going to the pub. But he felt that some music was needed. He wanted a semblance of normality when Rita arrived. Silence wasn't him.

He went through his record collection from A to Z. Nothing appealed. Everything came with strings attached. Memories that were his or theirs. Theirs were out. And his without her, well, they were him alone, yes, without her. He needed something unobtrusive, perhaps instrumental. He came across *Wish you were here* and unthinkingly considered it. Then he realised the title and heard the title song in his head. Shit. How could he be so stupid? Yet, he smiled.

Andrea had introduced him to Pink Floyd's *Dark side of the moon*. He had loved the car crash. Expecting more of the same he had bought *Wish you were here*. He hardly played either of them now.

There was nothing. So he risked it and switched on the tuner. The enthusiastic babbling of the DJ shattered the silence in flat. Kevin turned the volume down to barely audible.

He collected up the pen and paper from the dining table. Would he ever get his letter to his aunt written?

His relationship with Rita was an on and off affair. But not like that with Beryl. Rita was virtually housebound by her son Justin. So she was often left to plead for him to come over. She would cook. Then she knew someone who supplied her with pirate videos and she offered him a video evening with a latest blockbuster. And he went. More often than not Justin was already in bed. Twice, after a meal Kevin had read him a bedside story. Kevin had four siblings so he knew how to handle children. And yet Rita always tried to keep Justin out of the way.

He wanted to finish with her. But like Beryl, their sex was good. They'd found their common ground. Rita was a spider and he was caught in her web. "Go for it, Rita." Ah, of course he was a willing victim.

He wasn't up to giving her the boot now. He wasn't sure he could handle anything. Emotionally he was a wreck.

Maybe the mother in her would offer him comfort. If she was coming for sex, well, she was in for a big surprise. But he couldn't believe that she would dare.

When the doorbell rang he nearly jumped out of his skin.

"Shit," he cursed. "Calm down."

He went to the intercom and simply buzzed the house door open. He dared a look in the mirror. And although he didn't want to, he found himself searching out the sorrow in his eyes.

"You know, you've got sad eyes, Beryl."

"So have you."

The knock on the flat door made him start like a frightened animal. He took a deep breath as if he were about to go underwater.

When he opened the door Rita stormed in and immediately embraced him. "Oh, Kevin."

He hugged her too, but he didn't feel anything, merely her handbag tapping his back. He just wanted to close the flat door. Her perfume wasn't unpleasant, but alien. It reminded him of his childhood and being forced to take the hugs and kisses from powdered aunts.

She disengaged herself, but held his arms pinned to his side so that she could look into his face. He allowed her a glance and a slanted smile.

"I'm okay," he said.

She had to accept this and left him to close the door. She placed her handbag next to the telephone, took off her three-quarter-length leather jacket and hung it on the wall peg.

"It stopped raining," he said.

"Yes." She was surveying the flat and he realised that it was her first time here. Yet, he suspected she was searching for evidence of another woman. In any case he was glad she wasn't scrutinising him.

"You want a drink?" She was wearing sprayed-on stonewash jeans and a white blouse. The top button was open to reveal the rod-like bones of her neck.

"Tea."

"Okay. You want to look around?"

"Yes."

"Help yourself. You won't get lost. Lounge, dining room, living room, you name it." He pointed to the doors. "Bathroom-toilet and sports room." It was reflex to name the bedroom so. She smiled, but not sincerely. "Kitchen," he said, gesturing and heading towards it.

Once there he filled and started the kettle. He heard her opening and closing doors. She appeared a moment later.

She stayed at the entrance, leaning against the doorframe.

"Not bad," she said.

He nodded and they were silent for a while.

"You want to talk about it?" she asked.

"Not really."

Silence.

"Later maybe," she said, quietly.

He looked over at her. She looked as gorgeous as ever. The light from the kitchen window brought out the reddish sheen to her dark hair. Her eyes bore into him. They were like pieces of blue ice. Then he noticed her blouse. A further two buttons had been underdone.

Kevin steeled himself against her.

She was about four years older than him. She would only have been in her early teens in the "Summer of love". Yet, she belonged to that era. She was of a different generation. Dope smoking was an integral part of her. She had told him that she would give it up if he wanted. But he said he didn't mind. He just didn't want to get into it himself. And so she never smoked in his presence.

Martin and his friends Grub and Digger had taken Kevin stock car racing. After a fantastic day they had returned to Grub's place where cold beer began to round off a dry, gritty, exhilarating day. Grub, Digger and Martin were smokers, but despite the smoke Kevin was happy to be in their company. They were older than him. And they were street-wise. Perhaps they regarded him as their protégé.

"That's enough beer," said Grub. "I'm getting full."

"What have you got?" Martin asked.

"The usual shit."

"Sit over there, Kev," said Digger. "Then we won't have to keep getting up."

And Kevin had accepted the joint when it was passed to him. He drew deep and concentrated on not coughing. His eyes burned and so he also had to contend with holding back his tears. He didn't enjoy the experience. He didn't feel high, he just felt out of it. With alcohol he knew where he was.

"You weren't expecting your ex to turn up?"

"No. It was a complete surprise." Rita and her husband appeared to have broken up amicably. There were sometimes accusations of unreliability, but by and large it worked.

"Justin was overjoyed. A circus is something special for a kid. I was going to take him to the park this afternoon. I'm glad I didn't. That rain would have caught us."

"It caught me."

"That's why you were watching the towel dry."

"In one."

"Yeah. It's not been a great summer, has it?"

It still remained light until about nine or so, but the long days and beer garden evenings were losing out to the chill and darkness.

"You got yourself a video," she said.

"Yeah." Although he had planned the evening, he found himself asking her. "You want to watch it?"

"What is it?"

"American Werewolf in London."

"I've seen it."

"Any good?"

"Yes. But I don't fancy it now. The special effects are great. Him changing into a werewolf. And it's funny too. Him waking up in the zoo and -"

"Okay. Don't tell me the story."

"You'll enjoy it."

The kettle clicked off and Kevin poured the water onto the tea bags in the mugs.

Rita opened the fridge. "You should let me do this. Go and sit down."

"I'm okay."

She came over with the milk whilst he played yo-yo with the tea bags. "This mine?" she asked.

"Whichever you want." She chose the nearest mug and poured in the milk. He drank his black without sugar, just like his coffee.

After dropping their tea bags into the flip-top bin they took their drinks back to the lounge, placed them on the coffee table and sat on the sofa.

"Are you going to work tomorrow?" she asked.

"Of course." It never occurred to him not to go into work.

He didn't lean back, but remained poised on the edge of the cushion, as if he was about to pick up his mug. Was she watching him? He knew she was struggling. Part of him wanted to make it easy for her. Yet, he remained inaccessible.

"There's not a lot I can say," she said.

He nodded.

"Do you want me to be quiet? We could sit in silence for a while."

He didn't know, but he didn't want to shrug his shoulders like a little boy. "Yeah."

For some reason he thought of Helen. He felt as if he were cheating on her. But he wasn't. He was seeing her, but he wasn't going out with her. Was he besotted or fascinated? Probably a little of both. And yet, something essential was missing. Rita had it. Was it the ability to flirt? Or was it sexiness? Either way Kevin was interested and yes, aroused. But it wasn't enough. She was too tame. Rita would say lame. Only if Helen could be a bit more like Rita.

ABC

I admit to throwing the first stone
But you opened up with a Kalashnikov
It's a skirmish we cannot condone
But the price of being together
Is small compared with being lonely
And if "I love you" is our motto
Would it be wrong to question
Why we are walking on tiptoe

Admit we may have been mistaken
Expecting "happy ever after" to be true
We were simply overtaken by something long overdue
And bedside stories read by Mum or Dad
Didn't prepare us for these reds and blues

*This is our heaven, occasional he**l***
*So let us pause for a seasonal phot**o***
*And for the Cause raise that Moloto**v***
*A toast: forever friend, sometimes fo**e***

Rita leaned forward and cautiously picked up her mug. She brought it to her lips and blew delicately across the surface of the liquid.

Her movement made him look at her. He saw the juicy pursing of her lips; noticed the single pearl earring bedded in her earlobe. And he remembered her perfume and saw through the buckle in her blouse the fine lace of her white bra.

"I'm sorry," he whispered.

She smiled. But she looked fed up or disappointed.

Rock your baby, by George McCrae, started playing on the radio. And again he was propelled into the past.

"I remember dancing to this in the discos," he said. She sipped her tea, listening to him intently. He smiled. "I used to wear a white suit back then." He picked up his tea and took a tentative sip. "That was before John Travolta came out in one in Saturday Night Fever. After that I couldn't wear it any more."

"I'm sure you looked good," she said.

Yes he had: in his stacks, flares and wide-collared shirts. All that was missing was a medallion. All of it was laughable now. Ah, but back then, he was the bee's knees.

Kevin put his tea down and before he turned to her she put hers down too. He looked at her and she looked back. She had been waiting for him to turn to her. Her white bra peeked at him and when he looked into her eyes, her smile told him she knew what he had seen. Not only this, but also that she was pleased that he had noticed her. Her lips parted slightly. She was waiting for him to make a move. But he didn't want to make a move. And then, he wanted her comfort, her love. But not her body. And yes, her body. But no. The movement between his legs appalled and excited him. And still she made no move. The moment was filled to the brim with telepathic communication. But then this was not real communication; it was a mantra. Come on. Come on. Her eyes, often so hard, were cool pools, soft, waiting. They were full of tenderness. In her smile, the wetness of her lips, wet with tea, wet with yearning, was the real Rita: the woman with the vociferous sexual appetite. The starved before a feast. He hesitated. His mind said he needed comfort, his body said he wanted more.

He averted his eyes and saw the mounds of her breasts again. The index finger of her left hand gave a minuscule twitch. But of course he had to make the first move. Sitting was becoming painful. His cock had always been independent of him. It had a life of its own. Sandra had christened it Nick. He didn't know why. Perhaps because it rhymed with prick. Yes, Nick had a life of its own; many a morning he would be up before him, standing to attention.

He met her eyes again. This time the hardness appeared to have returned. The smile was fixed, almost diabolical. In the hardness of her eyes was either challenge or retreat. He wasn't sure. Whichever, he saw his hand reach up to the far side of her face, rising to the challenge or to halt the retreat. A great tension left her shoulders and she swooned. Before his palm reached her cheek she had turned her head and kiss it. Then she leaned towards him to allow his hand to travel round to the back of her neck. Her face approached his and he moved to her. The kiss was full and slow. Her cloying, intoxicating perfume increased the pain between his legs. They parted for a moment and she said huskily: "Oh, Kevin." Her arms were about him and the new kiss bordered on violence. She squeezed the life out of him and he reciprocated. They gasped and dived into each other. Tongues came out to fence, dart and lunge and wrestled. And their hands massaged their necks and backs.

    He began undoing the remaining buttons of her blouse as if his life depended upon it. Her fingers tugged at his T-shirt tucked in his jeans. There was no time to lose. He opened her blouse like curtains - the view was great - and helped her pull his T-shirt over his head. "What happened?" she asked quickly. He didn't understand until he saw her eyes looking at his bruise.

    "Garage accident," he said, fobbing her off with the same - albeit abridged - lie he'd given Helen yesterday.

    She shook herself out of her blouse and he fumbled with the clasp of her bra. She jerked his belt buckle tighter to release it. Her bra clasp snapped open and she hunched her shoulders so that he could take the straps and liberate her breasts. Then she sat up to lift her breasts and struggled with the top button of his jeans. He put a stop to her progress by taking up her breasts and engulfing her rigid nipples in turn with his mouth. He flicked his tongue over them.

    The aroma of flowers, rich flowers, deep red petals, heavy and overbearing assaulted his nostrils. She gave a hum, almost a moan, of delight. Then she pushed him away and went for the button of his jeans again. And he went for her jeans. She pulled in her stomach to assist him and he was pulling down her zip whilst she continued to struggle with his button. She all but gave up and lifted her buttocks to peel off her jeans. He got up and stood before her and then she had no trouble opening the button. She tore down his jeans and was pleased with the bulge in his boxer shorts. He stepped out of his jeans and she stood and pressed herself against him. He moved back a little, his shins pushing the coffee table away from the sofa. He wanted more room. It didn't matter if tea had slopped onto the surface. She reached up and embraced him and their mouths met again. He felt her fingers at his hips. A nail scratched him as she found the waistband of his underwear. Without breaking the embrace or the kiss he manoeuvred so that she could push his shorts beyond the point of no return. She broke the embrace and dropped to her knees. He wanted to free himself of the shorts at his ankles, but could only throw his head back as she grabbed his engorged piece and took it into her mouth. He looked down at her and feebly held her head, feeling the pearl earrings on his little fingers. Now it was his turn to hum with pleasure.

Rita moved her head back and forth, her tongue circled and twisted. Kevin wanted to explode and grabbed her by the shoulders. He helped her up and moved her back towards the sofa, stepping out of his shorts. He grabbed her flimsy knickers and violently jerked them downwards. Unlike his shorts, they needed guiding all the way down; they even caught on the sheen of her slender legs. She freed a leg before falling back onto the sofa. She kept a foot on the floor, like the movies of old, opening herself to him by moving the other leg, bent at the knee, to the backrest of the sofa. She was beautiful. Her pose was a masterpiece. He fell upon her. And eased himself into her and she let out a gasp of elation.

He moved slowly at first, enjoying her relish. Her hands were all over his back. And then her nails came out and she scratched him. And he jerked more energetically. Soon she was tearing at his back and he dug into her ever more violently. Then he broke the rhythm. He lifted himself away, but remained inside her. His back was on fire. "Don't stop," she pleaded.

She was smiling, and she was completely transported. She was there and yet far away, drowning in the depths of the awakened pleasure within herself. He descended and she lifted her foot off the floor. He grabbed her wrists and pushed her hands, with those terrible claws, above her head. Then he kissed her neck and moved down her chest. But he couldn't reach her breasts without leaving her. So he released an arm and allowed the fingers of her other hand to entwine his. With his free hand he lifted a breast to his lips. Her free hand went to his buttocks. She pressed a cheek and he took up a slow rhythm.

    He left her breast and pushed his fingers into her hair. Her hand left his buttocks and went to his burning back. He stopped and stared at her. She looked at him. Her face was full of rapture. And he could see the pores of her skin. The make-up had fallen away. Her face was raw, exposed. And he remembered one of his first meetings with Helen. She had suggested going to an exhibition of old masters. Of course she had wanted mutual, public ground. The paintings had been photographic. The lighting perfect. The windows to the soul frozen for all to see. And then, close up, the paintings broke down. They became brush strokes and spots of paint. And so it was now with Rita. She broke down to skin and bone before him.

    She smiled and he remembered an earlier time with her. A time in the partial darkness of her bedroom, vague light coming from a gap in the curtains. Her eyes had disappeared, her lovely high cheekbones had hollowed out the sides of her face and for an instant he saw a skull. Her smile and show of teeth had been hideous. Beauty simply broke down at close range.

    "Let's do it on the table," she said, hoarsely. He shoved himself off her. They moved quickly. He was standing at the edge of the table inside her as soon as she had lifted herself onto it. At first she held him, then she leant back on her extended arms, before easing herself onto her elbows, her head tossed back, hair cascading upon the table, breasts moving to his beat. He slowed his pace to watch himself moving in and out of her.

    "Oh Kevin," she moaned.

    He increased the pace and felt a surge that was the precursor for losing control. So he looked about for distraction. He saw his buttocks in the mirror. Tried to listen to the radio, but couldn't hear it over her breathing.

"Ah," she cried as she lifted herself off her elbows.

"Okay?"

"Yeah." She reached up. And he bent to kiss her.

He felt her hands move across his stripped back. Perhaps she felt the damage because she moved to his biceps. After a moment of wandering with her nails, as if trying to find the right spot, she stopped. She dug into him painfully and he was forced to tense his biceps. He had once asked her about using her nails on him, especially on his biceps and she said she did it to take his mind off what he was doing.

He pressed her to him, using his knees to slip and rise up into her, but he couldn't tense his biceps for much longer. So he withdrew.

"Let's do it backwards," he said.

"Yes."

He stepped back and she hastily moved across the room and put on her heels. She returned to him and grabbed the back of a chair, offering him her backside. He found her and she fell further forward, her breasts hanging, wobbling with his pulse. He leant forward to scoop them up, but he couldn't move easily, so he reared up, placing his hands on her back.

"Oh Kevin, yes, yes, ..."

He felt another surge.

"Don't stop."

He wanted her to shut up.

"Only you."

"Shhhh."

"Mmmm," she said. "Hit me," she said thickly.

Everyone had a tick and this was Rita's. He slapped her buttocks and they juddered. She tensed gripping him tightly. He slapped her again. Her other buttock this time.

He wanted to scratch her, to tear at her back, to brand her with weals like she had branded him. His back still burnt. But his nails were dirt-rimmed stubs. He couldn't remember ever cutting them. As a kid he'd always bitten them down. Later the grime of work put a stop to that. But the nature of his job kept his nails worn down.

He slapped her again. Her hanging breasts rocked from side to side like bells.

He tensed against another surge. She felt it.

"Don't come," she said.

And then he was standing in the balance, teetering on the brink of exultation. Withdrawing or a change of pace was necessary and he wanted neither. He needed other thoughts, but his mind was suddenly flooded. He wanted to let go, but he didn't want it to end, for his sake and hers. Then something collapsed within him. He gave up.

"I can't," he whispered. He started pushing earnestly.

She darted a hand to herself and began rubbing. But she hardly had time. He exploded. She continued to touch herself, but without him she began to lose momentum. And then she gave up with a sigh.

Her disappointment showed in the sag of her shoulders.

He stepped back.

She turned.

"We've had better," she said.

"You want me to do something for you?"

"No," she said firmly.

She brushed passed him to the bathroom.

He turned towards his clothes and caught his stricken face in the mirror at the door. She had not alleviated his troubles. She had added to them.

He'd always waited for her: given her a good run for her money. They'd worked up the standard to this level. Anything less was unacceptable. Perhaps worrying.

Kevin pulled on his boxer shorts and picked up his tea. Some of it had spilt. He let drops fall from the bottom of his cup into the small puddle on the coffee table.

The toilet flushed.

He put his cup down near the puddle, knowing he'd make a ring, and went to the kitchen. There he squeezed out the washing-up sponge over the sink.

The sky was overcast again and far off, darker clouds promised more rain.

Back in the lounge he wiped the table with the sponge.

Rita appeared. She looked haggard: hair dishevelled, face somehow sagging.

He smiled as he took the sodden sponge, his other hand cupped underneath it, back to the kitchen sink. He knew she would have seen the awkwardness in his smile. He couldn't hide the fact that his lust for her had dissipated with the shedding of his seed.

Kevin felt her behind him before he turned from washing out the sponge. She was again at the entrance. She hadn't dressed, but she was clutching her handbag.

"Don't worry about it," she said. "You're upset."

Did she expect him to apologise? He knew he could do better. More importantly, she knew he could do better. And anyway, he'd offered to do something for her.

He didn't say anything. Instead he dried his hands on the tea towel.

She made a noise: a kind of huff. Then she turned and went into the bathroom.

"You want something to eat?" he called.

"What have you got?" she asked distractedly.

"Digestives."

She was silent for a time. "Okay."

He went to the cupboard. The packet was already open. He took the top biscuit and bit it. It wasn't too soft, which meant that the others would be acceptably crisp. He fingered out five onto a tea plate and took them to the coffee table.

The clock showed 17:35. Maybe she had wanted to eat properly. But he didn't have anything in; just three eggs, enough for an omelette.

By the time she came out he was on his second biscuit and he had put on his T-shirt.

She had hastily made up her face. The haggardness was

replaced by hardness. She looked severe, almost poker-faced. Her eyes were hostile, lips determined, nose like a beak, brow hard.

Kevin couldn't gauge her in the silence in which she dressed before him. She didn't turn away from him as she dipped her breasts into her bra, but she didn't face him either. She clipped it closed and then scooped up her knickers and pulled them on. Finally she put on her blouse before falling onto the sofa next to him.

In the heat of the moment he had noticed that her underwear was new or at least he'd never seen it before. He had made a mental note to ask her about it, but now he couldn't. He was slightly miffed that she'd arrived wearing it, knowing how he could be feeling.

She leaned forward, ate a biscuit and drank her tea. He didn't lean forward. He looked beyond her into the blank face of the television set. He could make out her face, but not her expression.

"I -" he began quietly, but his mouth was dry because of the biscuit. "I heard this morning." She didn't tense, but she remained still. As if to move would break some kind of spell. "Sandra was killed on Wednesday night." He was quiet, but she did not move. So he leaned forward. "She got run over." He picked up his tea.

She put a hand on his bare knee. He glanced down at her slender fingers, her mother of pearl talons.

"How long ago were you together?"

"We, er, broke up, over two years ago."

"That's a long time ago."

He bristled. His silence told her she had pushed the wrong button.

"My husband and I separated around then. But the break-up started long before that. It was drawn out and terrible."

Where was she coming from?

"It's not quite the same thing," he said.

"I'm not saying it is."

"Then -"

"I was trying to talk about pain."

They were silent. He listened to the radio continuing on its merry way.

"She meant a lot to you."

You don't say, he thought.

"Kevin, you look wrecked. Why don't we go and lie on the bed?" She had the sense not to move her hand on his knee.

"No."

"I have to be back by eight."

He nodded.

"Kevin, look at me."

He turned and saw her hurt and concerned face. She looked as if she was going to cry. Her face implored him to return to her. And he then realised that he had been shutting her out.

She moved her far hand to his neck and he let himself lean towards her for a kiss.

There was tenderness in this kiss. And that was how he wanted it. She was broken before him. So he was surprised when they disengaged and she slowly got up. "Come on," she said, extending a hand towards him.

Maybe he was the broken one.

He looked at her hand and then up at her smiling face. The light brought out the reddish hue of her hair. She was statuesque.

His smile was lopsided as he accepted her hand and pushed himself off the sofa.

She led him to the bedroom and he followed sheepishly. She manoeuvred him and helped him lie down as if he were an old man. Then she went round to the other side of the bed and lay down beside him.

Kevin stared at the ceiling and she curled up to him, a hand on his chest. "Relax," she said. "Close your eyes."

They were silent for some time.

"Do you want me to massage you?"

"No," he said, quietly.

She didn't say anything and he began to relax. Eventually he felt himself sinking. Unconsciousness lapped at the edges of his mind before engulfing him completely.

A moment later he began resurfacing. At first his mind was slow to register where he was or what had happened before going to sleep.

Her voice was a shock and he froze. "You've been asleep for nearly an hour."

Rita was stroking his chest under his T-shirt. This had brought him back. He squinted. The light was brutal. He closed his eyes again.

She knew he found the fingering of his nipples irritating, but she still brushed over them. She moved down to his stomach and stroked him there, moving across his waist.

He told himself to relax and actively controlled his breathing.

Her hand came to his chest again, wandered for a while, before dropping back down to his stomach and then a little further, to skim the waistband of his boxer shorts. Then she was rubbing his belly.

Rita shifted closer to him and he felt her breath on his cheek, smelt her perfume again. She kissed him.

Then she was nibbling an earlobe.

Although he was shocked he kept his eyes closed.

Her hand was exploring his waistband, teasing the pubic hair. Then her head was on his chest and he was forced to breathe through her hair. It smelt pungent and artificial. Her hand could now venture further, but she didn't slip it under his waistband. Instead she stroked his thigh.

Kevin didn't know what do. He was enjoying her attentions, but not where they might be taking him. Or maybe he didn't mind.

She said something, but he didn't catch it.

"What?" His voice was cracked.

"It's always better the second time." Her hand was now massaging him through his boxer shorts.

He was stunned. How could she misjudge him?

He felt stirrings. Had she misjudged him? Mentally, yes. Physically, apparently not. Nick was on the move.

Kevin's groan was taken as a signal and Rita sat up and pulled down his boxer shorts. She began to seriously titillate his genitals first with her nails and fingertips and then with her mouth. Was he ready? Or was it too soon?

Kevin stared at the strand of dust that hung from a point on the ceiling. It swayed. Such a strange stalactite.

Rita's efforts were engorging Nick. He was growing satisfyingly heavy. He wasn't quite hard enough but Rita tore off her knickers and mounted him. He welcomed her slick warmth. She pulled her blouse over her head as she moved over him and then she unclipped her bra. He pushed all his energy into his hips.

"Yes, yes," she said excitedly. Her mouth split with joy.

He saw the rhythmic flutter of her hair, felt her spread-eagled fingers touching his stomach, heard the squeak of the bedsprings, the crack of the wooden headboard, smelt sweat and sperm, but more than anything he watched the bounce of her breasts.

Then he saw the stalactite of dust dancing as if in a gale. And he marvelled that it didn't get torn off.

Nick was standing proud. And Kevin was proud of him.

Kevin relaxed. Nick didn't need his help. He began to think of other things.

He thought of her son at the circus with his Dad. And here he was screwing his mother. No. She was screwing him. And maybe Justin was laughing at the clowns. Or following a trapeze act. Or gaping at a fire-eater. And then in the same utter silence in which the incident had transpired, patches of the fire-eater's face caught fire.

"Kevin," Rita gasped.

Sandra had called him dish. And the dish had caught fire. In an instant.

Rita changed the pace by falling upon him for a violent

kiss. He met her kiss with equal violence and yet his heart wasn't in it. Her hips grinded against him. Nick was in the grip of a stranglehold. And he was being drowned. If she didn't start moving Nick would whither. He pushed her away.

In an instant.

"She didn't suffer," said Tim. "It was instant."

And there was no sound as a girl ran across the dark road. A hush as the car slammed into her. Absolute silence as Kevin watched the single fat tear roll down her face.

"What's wrong?" Rita asked.

Kevin returned. Despite Rita's efforts his penis had turned rubbery. He didn't have the energy. Something in his will was broken. Nick continued to shrivel.

"Kevin?" she said, finally coming to a stop.

"I can't," he said, without a trace of apology in his voice.

"Oh, for Christ's sake," she sighed loudly, rolling off him.

They lay side by side for a while. He didn't know how she felt. And he didn't care.

"What's wrong?"

"What do you think?" he said quietly.

"Don't tell me it's still this girl." He didn't reply. "What is it with you men?" He knew she was lumping him with her husband and some theory of hers about men's emotional ineptitude. It went something along the lines of men being like children in that they were short of a few stops on the way to emotional extremes. "You could do it before. Why not now? Why not for me?"

Still Rita hadn't read the menace in his silence.

"You just don't care. Do you?"

"I guess not," he said.

She was stunned. "You selfish git. You've had your fun."

"I didn't want it."

"Sure. That was obvious."

"I –"

"She dumped you, didn't she?"

"Button it, Rita."

He felt her go rigid. There was electricity in the air.

"Don't you talk to me like that. She dumped you and I can see why."

"You'd better leave," he said.

"You just used me."

"Ditto."

"What? You conceited, selfish bugger. You –"

"Get out, Rita," he said.

"You don't get rid of –"

"I said get out!" he roared.

The ensuing silence seemed to ring with his roar, like a deafening echo.

She didn't move.

"Kevin," she began quietly. "I, I'm sorry. I didn't mean it. I know you're upset. I -"

"I said get out," he said in a voice of quiet contempt.

"Don't be like that. Let me cook something for you. I –"

"I've never hit a woman before, but there's always a first time."

She was quiet. But still she didn't move. She was close to turning on the waterworks and he knew that they might work on him. "I'm going to the bathroom. When I come out I want you gone."

He gave her a moment to react, but she said nothing.

Kevin got up and without looking at her he went to the bathroom. He latched the door and stood looking at the shower curtain. Then the towel. But it was dry, so there was nothing to watch. After a while he heard her moving about. He tried to imagine what she was doing. Then he heard the flat door open. He let out a long slow breath. But he didn't hear the door close.

Then he heard her shoes clacking across the floor, getting louder until they stopped at the bathroom door. "You've blown it with me, Kevin," she said in a quivering but defiant voice. "I feel sorry for you. You've really lost the plot." She waited, before hissing: "So you can just fuck off and die."

The sound of her shoes on the floor retreated. Then, a second later, the flat door was slammed which such violence the whole building seemed to shudder.

Kevin waited. He didn't hear her descending the stairwell. But maybe he wouldn't. He listened for movement, but heard none. Could she be standing inside the flat at the door?

He eased back the latch and waited a moment before opening the door. He looked across the lounge. Their half-finished teas were still on the table. The tea plate held a digestive and a half.

Kevin wandered to the bedroom and absently pulled on his boxer shorts. Then he went into the kitchen. There he stood, wondering what to do next. He returned to the lounge and went to the window that overlooked the street. He couldn't see her.

The sky was darkening again. Maybe after getting chucked, she'd get pissed on too. He smiled. Had he chucked her? Or she him? It didn't really matter. It was done. And he'd wanted it done. Of course, he could have done without the verbal firework show.

He turned when he recognised a tune on the barely audible radio. He went over to check that he had heard correctly. Then he smiled and turned the volume up to let Kool and the Gang fill the room with *Celebration*. "Ha!" he exclaimed.

"Laugh? I almost bought a round," said Tony.

In the kitchen he checked the clock. It was 18:45. He should eat. But he couldn't be bothered with cooking, even if it was only beating up some eggs for an omelette.

The second time he remembered his mother being furious with him was when she caught him throwing eggshell into the dustbin. He'd been hungry and had stolen an egg from the fridge. He had heard that in Arabian lands it was so hot you could fry an egg on the ground. And it was a blistering summer's day. He cracked the egg on a piece of tin foil on the ground. But it didn't cook and he tipped it onto the dirt and stirred it out of existence with a stick.

He wasn't the only one who did such things. He also remembered his mother calling them all into the lounge. Whilst cleaning she had found a dusty raw potato behind the sofa. A single bite had been taken out of it. The size of the bite mark was not enough to betray the culprit. All of them denied taking it. And all of them were sent to bed without supper.

He could start watching the film. But it was too early. Seven thirty would be a good time. Then he could go to bed afterwards.

He returned to the lounge and finished his cold tea. He took the two mugs to the kitchen, tipped out the remnants and stood them in the bowl in the sink.

Kevin then returned to the bedroom. He opened the wardrobe and took out his black blazer. He didn't possess a suit. But he had this blazer and a pair of black trousers. They were both fine and wouldn't have to be taken to the dry cleaners. His white shirt would need ironing. He searched for and found his thin black tie. He didn't have many ties.

"Don't pull on my ties," he said.

But Sandra wasn't really listening. She was excited with anticipation.

And yes, they'd experimented. They'd gone together on sexual explorations.

"You've really lost the plot."

Maybe she was right. Maybe he'd been mourning long before Sandra's death.

He flopped onto the bed and stared at the hanging strand of dust.

His mind was too active for sleep. So he opened the bedside cabinet and took out the poetry book Helen had lent him.

Thoughts on the Third World

You thought you were sad
But you don't know sadness
You thought you were hungry
But you don't know hunger

You thought you were poor
But you don't know poverty
You thought you were happy
And yes you know happiness

Most of the poet's works were awful birthday card jingles. A bouncy series of words that didn't hold up under scrutiny. But this was thought-provoking.

Of course, some bugger was always worse off. Some unfortunate was being tortured or murdered. But Kevin reasoned that his pain was no less real. It was his very own pain. And he *was* being tortured. Even if he was the torturer. And yes, some part of him had been murdered. Even if he was the murderer. But wasn't circumstance the torturer? Wasn't circumstance the killer?

Kevin had long decided that Helen's poet was a brown head: a guy with his head up his arse.

He wanted to phone her and tell her that the guy was a brown head. Not in those words. But he knew he was still too angry. And maybe he'd use those words. But he was really phoning her for her sympathy and not to tell her about the book. She would be her demure self. And her shyness, which normally lent him a larger than life character, could now only infuriate him. It wasn't in her to offer him comfort. She didn't know how to. She only knew the brash, confident Kevin. She'd never seen this wounded animal. No. She wouldn't know what to do. It would be a mistake to call her.

Weariness began to overwhelm him. He yawned.

Then he pulled the quilt over his bare legs, but left his arms exposed. He didn't want to sleep for too long. But sleep he did.

His sleep was fitful. His mind tried to flood him with images and memories, but he was too exhausted to let them profoundly disturb him. Instead they irritated him.

When he woke it again took him a moment to realise where he was and what day it was.

His argument with Rita seemed as if it had happened yesterday. And his time in the pub was certainly not today. Perhaps it had all been a dream?

He felt stirrings. His penis was growing.

"Oh, for Christ's sake," said Rita.

"Yeah, Nick," he said aloud. "What are you playing at?"

He wondered about Rita. Rain tapped on the window. He was sorry they had finished. She was so sexy. And then he was relieved it was over. It was a loss nevertheless.

The book of poetry lay on the bed. He picked it up. Another few pages and he'd be finished.

I'm lying

I'm crying
I'm dying
Like you
It's true
I'm lying

Now what was that meant to mean? Selfishness? Self indulgence? Attention seeking? Me, me, me.

His father hadn't been lying.

"I don't feel any pain," his father announced. And Kevin was glad. He was relieved and appalled. In his emaciated state it was a wonder he had felt anything.

Kevin rolled over. He still felt tired, but knew that more sleep would mean he wouldn't sleep tonight. And he had work tomorrow.

The cloud of dust under the chest of drawers was again visible. As if it had a life of its own. Coming into the room probably mobilised it.

"Kevin," said Sandra, "you slob. I wanted to hoover here, but -"

"Vacuum clean."

"You know what I mean. But there was a cobweb on your

hoo- vacuum cleaner."

He had laughed.

"So? Don't tell me you want me to clean the vacuum cleaner?"

"Yes. You could do that. But if there is a cobweb then there's a spider." What was it with women and spiders? Sometimes he crushed them with the heel of his hand, fat ones with a piece of toilet paper, other times he caught them and set them free. Of course he didn't like it when they escaped his hand and scampered up his arm. Sandra screamed and almost fainted when that happened.

Kevin swung his legs off the bed and looked behind the door. The upright vacuum cleaner stood like a sentry. He couldn't see any cobwebs.

Rain tapped the window like impatient fingers.

He grabbed the machine. It was old and squeaked, but it was solid and it worked. He unwound the cloth-covered cord and plugged it in. After switching it on he methodically moved about the room, the wheels squealing through the woompf of the machine.

Actually he wasn't sure whether it worked. It was possible that it merely blew the dust into the air, allowing it to resettle elsewhere. He couldn't remember when he'd last changed the bag.

With the bedroom done, the dust under the chest of drawers either sucked up, or pushed further underneath, he moved into the lounge. He wanted to change the bed sheets and it was already seven thirty, so he did a poor cleaning job, merely going round the furniture.

Kevin packed the vacuum cleaner away and stripped the bed. He hated changing the bedding, almost as much as ironing. Even washing his clothes was better. Sitting in the laundrette was bearable simply because he could read or get the chance to chat-up a woman. He sometimes left the machine going and went to the pub.

He'd put the book of poetry next to his alarm clock.

Normally he hid it away inside the bedside cabinet. He picked it up, and checking the last pages, realised he'd read all the poems.

"Wank," he said quietly. And then he thought of his drunken effort last night: pure ranting.

The rain had abated.

He tapped the book in his hand and then took it to the telephone. There he dialled Helen's number. He knew she'd be in working. She'd said so yesterday. But -

She picked up after two rings. "Hallo?"

"Hi, it's me."

"Kevin?" she was surprised.

He was quiet for a moment. Why had he called her?

"Kevin?"

"Yeah. Sorry. I, er, finished your poetry book."

"Oh." Yeah, so what?

"I don't -"

"What's wrong?"

Yes, this wasn't him. He was strength in front of her. Confident and full of beans.

"I had -" He shouldn't "- some bad -" have phoned "- news, -" her "this morning."

She was silent and he realised he had told her nothing.

"An ex-girlfriend of mine was, erm, killed."

"I am sorry."

"Yeah, she was run over."

"Kevin, I'd, er, like to see you, but I haven't got the time. I told you I've got to get something done before next weekend. You -"

"It's okay." What had he expected?

She'd now heard him without his buoyant mask and he could hear the uncertainty in her voice. She didn't know this Kevin. And maybe she didn't like what was behind the mask. He shouldn't have phoned her.

"These things are sent to try us," she said.

Silence.

"To, er, make us appreciate life," she continued.

"I'll tell her sister and parents that at the funeral, shall I?"

He too was surprised by his venomous retort.

"I'm sorry," he said.

"It's all right. You're upset."

"Yeah. I'll have to get the book back to you." Then he perked up. "I'll call you, like we said. We'll meet Wednesday or Thursday for a drink."

"Yes, that'll be nice." Nice. What a weak ineffectual word. Like her. She had no spunk. Sandra had spunk. She hadn't been afraid to speak her mind. She'd stood up to him.

Then he heard his own voice using the same word in her presence.

"It's *nice* taking a walk," he said.

And: "How come a *nice* girl like you is not going out with someone?"

"It's just so *nice* to sit here in silence and watch the day. Some people miss it all. They just ruin it by talking. Going on and on and on -"

"Okay, speak to you soon, then," he said.

"Yes, take care."

"You too."

"Bye."

"Bye."

He hung up. He'd buggered that good and proper. He still wasn't sure why he'd phoned her. Comfort? Or confirmation of something?

"These things are sent to try us," she had said.

And who sent these things to try us? God? Pah. His father had believed in God. Once. "I don't know what I've done to deserve such pain." After that his father had felt abandoned.

Yonks ago they had an argument about religion when Kevin had admitted to not believing. "You'll be a heathen," said his Dad.

"Calling me names is not going to make me change my mind."

The death of his father kicked everything into touch.

Religion was a crutch to help you limp through life. And for those with a gammy leg it was fine.

"I'll call you, like we said. We'll meet Wednesday -" Wednesday was the funeral.

Kevin looked at Helen's book in his hand.

"What the fuck," he said. Satre, Hamsun, this poet. Helen had introduced him to them. He had not told her, but he had skipped wads of text, pages even. He'd told her he was a fast reader. That had scored him some points. Who reads this stuff nowadays? Students perhaps. To Kevin it was all simply entertainment and as such as lasting as fashion.

And philosophy? That was just brown heads thinking up empty platitudes. Where did it get them? They'd just ploughed the sea. They were as dead as he would be one day. I stink therefore I was. So what?

And history? History explained the present, just as his past made him what he was now. But did it help him? Could he fight it?

Of course Kevin knew his place. Philosophy, history, culture. He couldn't appreciate all this stuff. It was not important to him. His interest in it was mild to non-existent.

He remembered watching an animal programme on television with his brothers and sisters. They all liked nature programmes. It said that if a monkey could talk he would probably ask for a banana. Not because he was hungry. But because this was important to him. And some people lived from day to day, hand to mouth, with simple wants. And simple wants were more likely to be met. Contentment was attainable. But people always wanted more. So that was that.

Kevin went to the kitchen. It was 19:40. Definitely time for the film. Too late for his omelette? He checked the cupboard. There was a tin of salted peanuts. In the fridge was a nub of cheese. He should cook up an omelette, but he couldn't be bothered. It was too late.

He took a good bite out of the cheese and it was half gone. He stood and chewed it down. Then he popped in the remaining piece.

He grabbed a tumbler and the tin and returned to the lounge. After placing them on the coffee table he took a dining chair to the stereo. The radio was still playing and he switched it off. He stepped onto the chair and pulled down the Laphroaig cardboard tube from the top of the wall unit. He stepped down, put the box on the coffee table and returned the chair to the dining table.

He opened the box and pulled out the bottle of Johnnie Walker Black Label. It was three quarters full. After checking he had everything he needed he pushed the videocassette into his machine and switched on the television. After switching off the overhead light and switching on the standing lamp, he went back to the sofa, used the remote control to fast forward to the film, opened the tin of nuts, poured himself a good measure of whisky and sat back on the sofa, his feet up on the coffee table, the tin of nuts in his lap.

Once during the film, rain drummed on the window, otherwise he ate, watched and drank undisturbed. Within the first hour he drank half the bottle. Reason told him to stop, but the drinker said he was fine and there was so little left in the bottle that he might as well finish it. And so he did.

When the film came to an end just over an hour and a half later he let the credits run. The film had held his attention. It had eased the onslaught of memories. And yes he had enjoyed the film. Rita had been right. The special effects were great: especially David changing into a werewolf. The disintegration of his dead friend, Jack, did bring his father to mind. But the scene in the cinema, where David's victims suggested ways for him to take his own life, quickly dispelled these thoughts.

Yes, the gore and horror had been carefully orchestrated, so that only shock and humour were left.

He knew he should be drunk. Maybe he was. But he felt okay. Only when he began pressing the button on the remote control to stop and rewind the film did he know that he was drunk. The remote control didn't react to his efforts until he saw he had it the wrong way round: pointing to himself.

He got up, surprised by the stiffness in his legs. When he went to the television, his step was uncontrolled and he was annoyed. He switched off the television and left the video rewinding. At the coffee table he picked up the empty tin and lid, drained the dregs from the tumbler and then from the bottle itself. He carried it all to the kitchen.

"You've got work tomorrow," he said to himself. Or did he speak? Was it a thought?

"I'm fine," he said aloud, but his voice was a slur. "I'm not drunk," he said as precisely as possible.

"You've blown it with me, Kevin," Rita said in a quivering but defiant voice. "I feel sorry for you. You've really lost the plot."

Lost the plot? What was she going on about?

Then she hissed: "So you can just fuck off and die."

Original, real original.

"You too, Rita," he said almost incomprehensibly.

The bottle was placed next to the kettle, the tin was tossed in the bin, the tumbler went in the bowl in the sink. He fetched a sleever and put it under the cold tap. The rush of water filled and then overflowed the glass. Although he held it with two hands the sleever wobbled and water splashed into the sink as he leant forward to slurp it.

He drank as much as he could and topped it up.

Then he saw the sky beyond his reflection in the glass. It wasn't raining and daylight was losing out to the night. But although it was after nine it was still relatively bright. Maybe there was a rainbow somewhere.

"Where would you weigh a pie?" Mick had asked them.

"What?" Even the question was enigmatic. Pie scales?

Later, after lunch, he told them that you could do it over a rainbow.

Eh?

And Mick sang the title song from the Wizard of Oz. "Somewhere over a rainbow weigh a pie."

The sky was not spectacular, but dramatic. There was a bit of everything. Dark, light, grey, yellow, gold, even some red. So that it was hard to tell which way the weather was going to go.

To Kevin the sky was beautiful.

And Sandra would never see it.

He felt the water come to his eyes. Then just as when he'd been on the brink of coming with Rita, so here he hung in the balance. He grabbed the stainless steel sink for support. Looked down and then returned his blurred gaze to the clouds. The first tear to break free rolled quickly away. His mouth twisted into something of a silent scream and his reflection resembled Munch's painting. Then warm tears rolled down his face. He sobbed and shudders racked his body. A groan slipped out and then he moaned loudly.

He stood there and cried and cried, astounded that he couldn't stop. And he didn't want it to stop. He wanted it all out. All of it.

At one point he whispered: "Oh, Sandra." Otherwise he just sobbed.

Still crying he left the kitchen to the bathroom. He needed to blow his nose.

At the toilet he tore off a couple of strips of toilet paper and blew his nose. After throwing the sodden thing in the toilet he tore off another couple of strips and blew his nose again. This too went in the toilet. He used a further couple of sheets to wipe his nose.

"Merry Christmas," said Kevin after sneezing painfully into his napkin. The white linen, his mother's best, was bright red with blood.

Rosie shrieked when she saw it.

Kevin had been sitting in the toilet cubicle. Of course he heard the door open, the sound of voices from the pub suddenly grew. For a moment he heard nothing and assumed the newcomer had gone to the urinals.

With an almighty crash the door was kicked aside. Kevin looked up, thinking a drunkard had bashed into it, but all he saw was a fist. That first punch was a blinder. It dazed him good and proper. There were two of them and they laid into him the best they could in the confined space. He managed to shout: "You've got the wrong bloke." But they probably didn't hear him. And with his trousers round his legs there was no way he was coming out like a windmill. All he could do was curl up and make sure he didn't sink to the floor. Oh, and they kicked him, trying to get his head, but hitting his shoulders, arms, sides and grazing the backs of his hands. Then they were away. Scarpering before he dare look up.

He was at the sink, washing his face, the backs of his sore hands, when his mate came in. He quickly stifled his sobs and told him what had happened.

Ha. Beaten up on his home turf. All he had wanted was to meet his old school pal for a quiet drink before Christmas lunch with his family. Of course his Dad wanted to come back to the pub and find the culprits. And his parents didn't quite believe him when he said he didn't know why he had been attacked. Mistaken identity was the best he could come up with.

Kevin flushed the toilet and looked in the mirror. His face was puffy. He wiped his eyes with the back of his hands. Then he tried to smile. But the sadness was overwhelming. He forced another smile and it was better.

He wearily squeezed toothpaste onto this brush. After brushing his teeth and his tongue, he switched off the standing lamp in the lounge and returned to the kitchen to fetch his sleever of water. At the sink he drank some more water. The sky had changed. The drama was gone, like drawn theatre curtains the clouds had closed.

Kevin filled the sleever as much as possible and went to bed.

His head was a motorway and there'd been an accident. Emergency bells were ringing. Pain stabbed his head like hot needles as he groped for the alarm clock. Meagre early morning daylight seeped over the top of the curtain rail.

Kevin felt awful. Worse than that: he felt poisoned. He'd woken twice in the night. The first time he'd gulped water. The second time he staggered to the toilet and returned and gulped more water. Yet, even now he felt parched. He lay there, too exhausted to do anything about it. Eventually he drank the remaining water.

If he dreamt he no longer remembered his dreams. When he had been conscious, traipsing back and forth to the toilet or fumbling for the glass of water, his mind had spun images, and he felt as if he was hallucinating. Mercifully, fatigue came to his rescue.

Nick was up before him.

He hauled himself out of bed. His stomach followed a second or two later. His head was in pain. Real pain. A vice was crushing his skull and the silence buzzed in his ears.

At the toilet he thought of sex with Rita, but he was too knackered to pull one off. So he eased Nick down like pushing the branch of a tree and waited.

In the kitchen the sight of the empty whisky bottle next to the kettle tightened his stomach. He groaned. He checked the kettle and switched it on. Then he returned to the bathroom, shaved and climbed into the bath like an old man. The sound of the curtain rings on the rail was horrid.

He turned the taps to mix the water and checked the temperature of the water with a foot. When he was happy he turned the lever to shower. The water standing in the tube was cold and as always it was a shock. But the warm water quickly followed. His back protested. It was sore and the skin was tight. He remembered Rita's clawing and was momentarily aroused.

After washing he dried himself and went back the bedroom, where he put on his watch, clean boxer shorts, socks, a

T-shirt and jeans. He dumped his clothing from yesterday in the wickerwork wash basket in the bathroom.

Back in the kitchen he made himself a coffee, topping up the boiled water from the kettle with cold from the tap. He sipped it. The thought of eating didn't appeal. The thought of working was worse.

Kevin finished his coffee at the kitchen window.

Then he returned to the bedroom and picked out the gold bracelet with his name engraved on it. Normally he didn't bother with jewellery for work. There was no point. He'd have to dump it in his locker when he got into his overall.

Before leaving he stuffed his wallet in the back pocket of his jeans. He could need his driver's license.

The sun was up, but low and it was quite cold, especially in the shadows.

He got in his car, switched on the engine and the radio and drove down the hill. The six-thirty news went on about some discotheque stabbing. A kid had intervened in some brawl and got himself killed. Innocents hit again.

Yes, death was everywhere. It could happen to anyone at any time.

He joined the main road and shuffled with the rest of the traffic. Accelerate, brake. Sometimes he got into third gear but the occasions were rare.

And what would they say about him when he was pushing up daisies? He was a great guy, a bastard, full of life, conceited git, lost, sad, easy-going, happy, cruel, considerate, soft, hard... Yes, he was all these things. He was also different things to different people.

And what was life? But a journey towards death?

His Dad had said: "be happy." But he could just as well have said: "Live each day as if it were your last."

And on Saturday Helen had said: "Every day should be a celebration."

He had laughed and she had questioned his laughter.

"It just seemed like a naff thing to say," he had scoffed.

"I love you, Dad," he managed. There, it was said. And he was glad he had said it. Why had it been so hard?

He recalled yesterday's walk with Helen and the play of light on the cottage wall, the great sense of peace, of getting off the merry-go-round. Was it all merely the eye of the storm?

"You made me feel cheap," said Andrea. Yes, he had. What a fool. What a waste.

Pissing in an empty milk bottle, like a dog marking territory that didn't belong to him.

Before Sandra reached the bend and disappeared out of sight she fumbled with the skimpy bikini top fluttering in her face, her other arm trying to balance and cover her breasts. "Keeeeeviiiin, yoooouu baaaastaaaard."

Then she was gone.

At the garage he parked on the street rather than in the yard. In the yard he could get boxed in.

As he walked into the garage, making a b-line for the stairs to Mick's office, returning morning greetings to those that were already there, he had second thoughts about asking for the day off.

He hoped Mick wasn't sitting behind a mountain of paperwork. At this time he'd be sorting out the work chits, but if he had some accounts to prepare for the accountant then he'd be especially grouchy.

But Mick was a good egg. During Kevin's first week at the garage he'd found himself standing alongside Mick at one of the two urinals. Kevin found that he couldn't go. He stood there wondering whether his boss thought he was there simply to skive. So Kevin forced himself. The result of his exertion was a ripping fart. Kevin blanched. Mick zipped up and without looking Kevin's way, he said: "Drop something there, Kev?"

Kevin climbed the wooden steps up to Mick's office. He knocked on the door even though it was open.

"Morning, Mick."

Mick looked up. He was sorting out the work chits: tasks for the day, estimating their duration and allocating the lads.

"Morning, Kev. You look as if you had an argument with the back of a bus." Mick smiled. "Demanding was she?"

Kevin grinned. "Yeah, her name's Johnnie Walker."

"That what you call her?"

"Don't make me laugh, Mick." He knew his smile was twisted.

"What up?"

"I'd like the day off. I don't think I can work." The smile was disappearing, just his twisted expression remained.

"Oh?" Mick put down the chit he held in his hand. "You want to close the door?"

Kevin closed the door and took the visitor's seat on the other side of the desk.

"I, er, had some bad news yesterday. An ex-girlfriend of mine was killed."

"That's terrible. I'm sorry. What happened?"

"A drunk driver got her."

"It wasn't a hit and run, was it?"

"No. They got him."

"Good."

"Did I know her?"

"Sandra."

Mick thought. "Yes, I think I remember her." After a moment he said: "Of course you can have the day off."

"The funeral's on Wednesday. I'll need the afternoon off."

"No problem. You sure you don't want to take the next few days off and come in on Thursday?"

"Yeah I'm sure. I'll be in tomorrow. I just need to get my head together."

"Come in when you're ready."

"Thanks, Mick."

Mick nodded.

"You could have phoned, but I appreciate you coming in. You want me to tell the lads?"

"Yeah. Why not?"

Mick nodded again.

Kevin got up. "Leave the door open," said Mick, picking up the chit.

As he walked out of the garage, looking neither left nor right, he felt Chris's stare. Out of the corner of his eye he saw Snotridge gooing up the top of a carburettor in his hand.

Back outside he felt relieved. The day now stretched before him. He climbed into his car and drove to Sainsbury's. There he shopped like a zombie.

Then he was back in the flat. After packing away his purchases he took a cup of coffee and a packet of chocolate digestives to the coffee table. He sat on the sofa and ate and drank. His headache was present but receding.

The Laphroaig box was still on the table. He'd kept it as the beginning of some whisky box collection. Now he would to throw it away.

Eventually he got up and put his sports kit together. A session at the gym would blast away any remnants of the headache.

He then went to the phone and pulled out the phone book. He found the number and dialled.

"Good morning. Could you tell me where I could find out about night classes? Yes. Subject? Erm, German. No, for beginners." He'd phone Kurt tonight. That'd surprise him. "Yes. Okay." He picked up the pen and wrote the telephone number the speaker gave him on his pad of paper. "Yeah. Thanks." Yes, he'd miss the treasure hunts too. "Bye. Wh- Yeah. *Auf Wiedersehen.*"

www.ingramcontent.com/pod-product-compliance
Ingram Content Group UK Ltd.
Pitfield, Milton Keynes, MK11 3LW, UK
UKHW041436180426
11947UKWH00007B/473